A Smith Brothers Novel

The Eye of Quang Chi

by Fred Adams Jr.

AIRSHIP 27 PRODUCTIONS

The Eye of Quang Chi
© 2017 Fred Adams Jr.

Published by Airship 27 Productions
www.airship27.com
www.airship27hangar.com

Interior and cover illustrations © 2017 Morgan Fitzsimons

Editor: Ron Fortier
Associate Editor: Jaime Ramos
Marketing and Promotions Manager: Michael Vance
Production and design by Rob Davis

ISBN-10: 1-946183-20-2
ISBN-13: 978-1-946183-20-0

Printed in the United States of America

10 9 8 7 6 5 4 3 2 1

Midnight.

*T*he sonorous tolling of the clock in the San Francisco Custom House tower rang through the fog and echoed from the warehouses blocks away, making each ring a double note. Bailey smiled at the symbolism. "For whom the bell tolls," he whispered to no one.

Bailey was a killer, pure and simple. The refinements of his craft may have qualified him as an assassin in some circles, a falcon rather than an attack dog, but at bottom, a killer. He watched as one by one the lights went out in the ground floor windows of the Smith Brothers' mansion. Finally, a light burned in only one window on the third floor. There he would find his quarry. The Smith Brothers were creatures of habit.

The Smith mansion was a Painted Lady, magnificent in its sprawling Gothic grandeur, testimony to its owners' wealth. But Bailey studied the spires, the oriels, and the gingerbread for practical, not aesthetic concerns: handholds, footholds, entry and exit.

Time to go to work.

Bailey crossed the street and crept from shadow to shadow to the spear-point fence. He found a stone the size of his fist at its base and pitched it over the wrought-iron palings. It landed with a dull thud. Bailey counted to ten. No dogs came running, confirming his surveillance from the night before.

The killer took a quick look up and down the street, and seeing no one, pulled himself up and over the fence, dropping into the soft mulch of a bed of begonias on the other side. He crouched and listened. A dog barked, but it was two streets away. Staying in the shadows of the polled elms, he slipped to the back of the house where he would make his entry.

Beside a small porch that opened off the kitchen, Bailey found the rose trellis that climbed two full floors and colored the dark brick of the mansion blood red in the sun. Tonight, he thought, I will paint the inside the same color. Bailey slipped on leather gloves, black like the rest of his clothing, and began his ascent. He took his time and made little sound. The thorns stabbed him through his trousers and sweater, but he did not flinch.

Beside the trellis on the second floor, Bailey stepped onto the sill of a tall window. The day before, he had studied it from a distance through a telescope and saw it was unlatched. His luck held. He pressed upward on the sash and it slipped open an inch. In a moment he was standing in the upstairs hallway.

Bailey left the window open and crept to the broad staircase. No sound from below. Then from the floor above he heard music; a flute and a cello playing an adagio, perhaps Haydn, perhaps Chopin. Good. The music would cover his approach. It had taken him nearly an hour to reach his objective, but the job demanded his kind of stealth. Bailey reached under his sweater and took the revolver from its holster at the small of his back.

He took the steps one by one, walking at the outside of the staircase, close to the wall to avoid a telltale creak from a loose tread. When he reached the third floor hallway, he saw light from an open doorway. The music had changed. Now it was an allegro piece, *Eine Kleine Nachtmusik*. How apropos, thought Bailey. "A little night music." He peered around the frame of the double doorway and saw two silhouettes against the glow of the hearth, heads and shoulders above a settee, one playing a flute, the other cocked to the side at a cello.

He knew the shape of those heads, their crowns, their ears. He had studied his targets, the twin brothers as he always did preparing for a kill, as carefully as a geometer examines every angle of a complex polyhedron. Bailey raised the pistol and hesitated. Which to shoot first? It didn't matter. Both had their hands occupied and could not reach for a weapon in the second between one shot and the next.

Dexter or sinister? Bailey decided on the latter and took aim. His finger squeezed the trigger.

His shot was disrupted by an arm around his throat and the blade of a dagger piercing his back. Bailey's revolver boomed, but the bullet went wild. A vase on the mantel exploded. The knife hand sawed upward like a chef at a roast and Bailey's pistol clattered to the floor. He screamed as he clawed desperately behind him but could find no purchase. A quick slash across the throat, and the assassin poured the last bit of his life onto the polished oak floor.

The figure on the settee rose and turned in a slow, wheeling motion, its silhouette a solid mass against the firelight. A small man in a tuxedo turned the valve and the gaslight cast its glow on the tableau. "I apologize, sirs, that I did not detect the man before he got this far." He crouched by Bailey's body and wiped the blade of his dagger on the dead man's trouser leg.

The little Honduran rose and turned to his employers.

The Smith Brothers, Ming and Hong walked around the settee with the odd smooth shuffle necessitated by being conjoined at the chest. They stared down at the corpse of their would-be killer.

"I believe, Raphael," said Ming, "that your timing was impeccable."

"A shame about the vase," said Hong. "It was Third Dynasty."

The clock on the mantel struck one.

*D*ownstairs, the Brothers drank tea at the round table that rested in a nook off the kitchen. They sat in one of the broad settee-like chairs designed and built for their comfort. Head on, the brothers looked as if someone had set a mirror at an angle beside a single man. Their Oriental features crowned the starched collars and worsted suits of an Occidental world. Ming, the leftward of the twins, dropped an extra cube of sugar into his cup. "So, who do you think sent him?"

Hong shook his head. "You'll kill us both with all that sugar and no one will need to hire an assassin." He frowned. "This was no run-of-the-mill street thug. Darby will find out who he is soon enough, and that will give us a better idea who his employer may be."

Ming stroked his pointed beard. "It was surely an enemy with a lot of money. That narrows the list to a hundred or so people in the city."

"And a hundred or so out of it if you include the whole Bay Area."

"And a dozen gangs of pirates."

"And a few members of the police department."

Ming and Hong were the sons of Reginald Smith, a British trader who, through his wits and his determination, created an importing empire, The Oriental Trade Consortium. He irritated San Francisco's business community with his upstart success and scandalized the city's elite society by marrying a beautiful Chinese woman, Ling-Tao, the daughter of a noble family.

When Ling-Tao died soon after giving birth to the conjoined twins, Smith's grief was enormous and he threw himself into his work, leaving the care of his freakish sons to servants. The boys were joined at the chest by a thick bridge of flesh and bone and shared a heart and one lung. They might have spent the whole of their days locked away in Smith's mansion on the Bay if it hadn't been for Robert Fellowes.

An Oxford scholar, Fellowes was hired by Smith to tutor his five-year-old sons and give them a traditional British education. The imperious little man arrived in San Francisco to find a pair of bright, inquisitive minds that had the misfortune of resting in one awkward body. On the second week of his employment, he barged into Smith's study over the remonstrations of Barrows, the butler.

"Your treatment of your sons borders on the verge of the criminal," Fellowes said in a voice that would freeze brandy.

Reginald Smith, accustomed to yes-men and sycophants, was taken aback. "What?" he sputtered, "Are you mad? They enjoy the very best of everything."

"They enjoy the best food, clothing and shelter, but they cannot enjoy the world. You keep them locked away in this mansion like birds in a comfortable cage."

"I am protecting them from a world that would ridicule and harm them."

"And when they are adults? Will you do so for their entire proverbial seventy or eighty years? Hong and Ming have brilliant minds, and great potential," Fellowes pointed an accusing finger at Smith, "which you stifle by making them think there is no world beyond your sphere. By coddling them and protecting them, you weaken them. They need to be taught to live in the whole world, not just your little demesne."

Reginald Smith was speechless. No one in his memory had ever spoken thus to him and escaped unpunished. Seizing the moment, Fellowes said, "My conscience will not allow me to perpetuate this travesty one more day. If I am to remain in your employ, sir, I must have a free hand to train Hong and Ming in every way to make them capable of navigating a difficult life on their own strength. For you, sir, cost is no consideration; the only impediment to Ming and Hong's independence is your weak will."

Smith's immediate inclination was to have Fellowes thrown into the street for his impertinence, but Fellowes stared him straight in the eye and said, "Ming and Hong are neither a shame nor a punishment, sir; they are human. Let them truly live."

Fellowes presented a bold plan to Smith: develop a regimen of total education for the boys with the goal of preparing them to function in society. Smith gave his assent, and soon, Fellowes was using his employer's considerable resources to prepare Ming and Hong to live fully in the world outside the mansion.

Fellowes said. "Defects of birth that would have had the boys burned as the spawn of witches in the past now inspire curiosity rather than fear. Ming and Hong have the good fortune to have been born to a wealthy father who can afford to teach them to make the most of the gifts God has given them."

The twins learned mathematics, chemistry, and biology as well as philosophy, history, and languages, but they learned much more than academic subjects. Their training included physical education to make them strong and gymnastics to develop coordination within the bounds of their condition. Fellowes brought in pugilists to teach them boxing, sharpshooters to teach them marksmanship, and a ballet diva to choreograph the movement of four feet to make grace of clumsiness.

Ming and Hong eagerly rose to each new challenge, learning quickly and persevering when their conjunction made a task difficult. When it came time to take them outside the mansion, Fellowes argued against a closed carriage. "It's nothing more than another cage on wheels," he argued to Smith. "Let them see the world, and let the world see them."

And what the world saw was a pair of young boys, wide-eyed and eager to take in everything the world had to offer. The twins rode with Fellowes on one side, and at Fellowes' insistence, their father on the other through San Francisco's streets. As Reginald Smith saw the delight and excitement in the faces of his sons at every new discovery, his eyes filled with tears. He never questioned Fellowes' judgment again.

Fellowes tutored the boys for twelve years. They came to call him Uncle Robert, and when his wife came from England to join him, she became Aunt Carrie. To his credit, Reginald Smith never felt a pang of jealousy at the affection his sons felt for the two of them, realizing that they were his sons' salvation. When their education was complete, Reginald pensioned Fellowes and at the boys' behest built him and his wife a house on a corner of the estate where he and Aunt Carrie could live the rest of their lives in comfort and where Ming and Hong could consult him at any time.

When they were twenty-three, Reginald died, leaving them Oriental Trading, and the brothers were ready to take control of the company. Ming and Hong became ruthless negotiators, and many a sharp trader found himself outnumbered literally and figuratively as the intuitive Ming debated terms while the pragmatic Hong's agile fingers flew over the abacus, supplying figures to back his brother's arguments.

Oriental Trading thrived, but the brothers, accustomed to challenge as a way of life, became bored with the workaday nature of company management. When a diabolically clever scheme of theft and embezzlement threatened to bankrupt Oriental Trading, Ming and Hong rose to that challenge as well, and unraveled a case that baffled San Francisco's Police Detectives and Pinkerton agents. They had found their true calling, investigation.

The twins delegated the operation of Oriental Trading and at the age of twenty-nine years opened a new business based in their mansion. A simple bronze plaque at the gate read "Smith Brothers: Investigation, Location, Restoration."

*K*enneth Darby strode to a rear gate in the fence around the Smith mansion. He shuddered in the chill drizzle and wished he had taken an umbrella when he left his flat an hour before. Darby was more compact than short, and his long overcoat hid shoulders broader than his waist.

He pulled a ring of keys from his pocket and unlocked the gate. Darby stepped into the formal garden behind the mansion and locked the gate behind him. The flagstone path to the house was lined with arbor vitae grown to head height, a dripping grey-green corridor. Another key opened the doors from the back porch to the kitchen. When the Smith Brothers built their house, all of the doors, stairways, and other accommodations were made double width to allow them to move freely.

Darby twisted the ornate brass bell knob, two rings, a pause then a third, knocked his derby against his fist to shake off the rain, and stepped inside. Before he had shucked off his coat, Raphael appeared behind him. "May I take your coat, Mister Darby?" he said.

Raphael's sudden appearance no longer startled Darby. The butler's gift of stealth was a primary asset. Raphael was only five feet tall and Darby easily outweighed him by fifty pounds, but Darby understood that Raphael could kill him as easily as clapping his hands.

The brothers had found their Honduran butler in the hold of a cargo ship while they were inspecting a load of coffee beans. Raphael had been the manservant of an assassinated dictator and had barely escaped with his life after killing his master's successor, along with three of his bodyguards. When the captain saw the stowaway, he whistled for a half dozen of his men to "teach the scoundrel a lesson."

The fight was brutal and short. At its end, five of the sailors lay on the floor of the hold; the sixth ran for help. Before he returned, the brothers stepped forward. Ming spoke to him in Spanish and their respective dialects were close enough for understanding. "Captain," said Ming, "We will pay this man's passage and any damages to your ship and crew. He will come with us."

The captain began to protest but stopped when Ming pulled a roll of bills from his pocket and began to peel off fifties and hundreds. By the time the crewman returned with reinforcements, the deal was sealed, and Raphael had become Ming and Hong's employee.

"Thank you, Raphael. Are the Brothers in their office?"

"No, sir, Messers Smith are at table. Come with me please." Darby followed Raphael through the kitchen and found his employers enjoying ham and eggs.

"Ah, Darby," said Ming. "Would you like something to eat? Perhaps Raphael could fix you an omelet."

Darby shook his head as he took a chair opposite the brothers. "No, thanks, I had breakfast already. But I will have some coffee." In seconds, Raphael appeared with a cup and saucer and poured from the decanter on the table. "What's up?"

"We need you to identify a person for us," said Hong. "But that can wait, Darby. Enjoy your coffee."

Kenneth Darby, formerly of the *San Francisco Chronicle*, was wooed away from the newspaper by the Smith Brothers because of his excellence and determination at research, particularly in the area of crime. He was as familiar with San Francisco's underworld as he was with his own family, and his ability to ferret out facts was unparalleled. "Was my report on Leyden Shipping adequate?"

"It was excellent," said Ming. Hong nodded agreement. "Those scoundrels underbid the competition out of desperation, hoping to save their company at our expense. You have saved us considerable cost and inconvenience once again."

Darby pulled a silver hip flask from his pocket and poured a shot of rye into his coffee. "They were a solid company once, but they overextended themselves; like swimming too far from shore to swim back."

"Yes," said Hong, "and they will likely be eaten by a shark." He turned his head to his brother. "Who do you think will buy Leyden out?"

"The likeliest candidate is Shackleford. He's been trying to corner the market for decades. I suppose Eastern Star is another possibility."

"I agree. Darby, please keep an eye on that matter for us."

Darby nodded and pulled a small leather bound notebook from his pocket. He quickly scrawled a note and finished his coffee. "So where do I find this fellow you want me to identify?"

"Upstairs," said Hong. Darby's eyebrows raised.

"We'll take the lift," said Ming. With a nod to each other the brothers pushed their chair away from the table and stood. Their conjointure pulled them forward slightly, but erect they stood just under five-and-a-half feet. Darby followed as they walked to the lift like soldiers marching in tandem, left feet then right with a precision that made no more noise than single footfalls.

The lift was a brass cage in a shaft built into one of the mansion's towers at its construction. Ming and Hong used the wide staircases as often as the lift, but enjoyed the convenience. At the third floor, they stepped from the cage. Raphael was waiting and led the way to the drawing room. He slid the pocket doors open, and in the dim light that filtered through the drapes, Darby saw a mound covered by a bloodied sheet on the parquet floor.

"Raphael interrupted this man as he was about to shoot us," said Ming. "Please see whether you know who he is."

Raphael pulled back the sheet and rolled the black-clad corpse over. Darby whistled. "That's Liam Bailey" he said. "He's imported talent, a professional assassin. Word is he charges five thousand dollars a kill. I guess whoever hired him paid double for the two of you."

"That would be foolish," said Ming. "One shot could kill us both."

"You are certain is it Bailey? You have met him before?"

"Not personally," said Darby, "but I never forget a face. I covered his trial in Sacramento for the murder of Diamonds Dunnigan. He walked on that one. Rumor is he's killed over fifty people, but that's probably an exaggeration. Someone must really want you dead."

"Ply your skills and see whether you can learn who hired him," said Hong.

"Are you going to call the police?"

Ming shook his head. "Better Mister Bailey's disappearance be a mystery to all, especially to those who sent him. That should give them pause before they try again. No reality is as unsettling as an uncertainty. Raphael will see to the body."

Darby had long ceased to marvel at the Brothers' blasé attitude toward attempts on their life, and it was life in the singular, since their shared heart meant that the death of one would quickly follow the death of the other. But their years of interfering with crime and criminals had made dangerous enemies for the Smith Brothers.

"I guess it goes with the territory," he had said once, and Hong replied after a brief pause for thought, "It is the territory."

"So, Darby," said Ming, "Learn what you can. Raphael will see you out."

Darby left the way he had come, and as he locked the garden gate, his mind was already turning over possibilities and sources.

*A*t ten o'clock, the gate bell rang. Raphael admitted the visitor, and as they walked up the carriage drive together, the brothers studied the guest from their office window. The man was Oriental, but like the brothers, clad in Western clothing. A queue snaked from beneath the flat brimmed hat on his head and a long overcoat draped his shoulders. He was just a little taller than Raphael, and his gait showed impatience and agitation.

Raphael brought him to the office and rapped lightly on the door. Without waiting for a response, he slid one of the pocket doors aside to admit the visitor. "Sirs," said Raphael, "Mister Sing Chung."

Ming and Hong rose from their chair. Raphael handed them a business card. Sing bowed from the waist. Raphael had taken his coat and hat, and Sing stood before them in a perfectly tailored suit, complete with a high starched collar and a pearl stickpin in his wine red stock.

"Please sit down, sir." Hong indicated a padded leather chair in front of the desk. Hong read the card: Sing Chung, Business Consultant. He passed it to his twin.

"Thank you, Mister Smith," Sing said with only the slightest trace of accent.

"I am Ming, and this is Hong. We appreciate refined demeanor, but it prevents confusion to use our first names when you address us."

"As you wish. Ming and Hong."

"Your English is quite good," said Hong.

"I had the good fortune to be educated in Hong Kong, where English is the language of commerce." The impatience he had shown when he did not know he was being watched had vanished, replaced by a suave, relaxed veneer.

"Your card says that you are a business consultant. What types of company do you serve?"

"I assist native Chinese who wish to establish businesses in San Francisco with all of the bureaucratic details they encounter with the City. I have found that the greatest obstacle is often a matter of language."

"And how may we be of service?" said Hong.

"I understand that you specialize in investigation and particularly in the finding of lost items. Recently, a crate from Hong Kong containing statuary belonging to my family disappeared from the docks as the freighter was being unloaded. The pieces were not especially valuable, but they have been in my family for generations and I am sure you understand my desire to have them back."

Hong opened a drawer of the desk and drew out a sheet of paper. "Please tell us, what is the name of the ship, and when did it dock?"

"The ship is the Parma Queen, and she docked two days ago."

"I know the Parma Queen and Michael Parnell, her captain," said Hong. "Has he been notified of the missing crate?"

"Yes. He has been of little help. I suspect that he finds the needs of a Chinaman less than pressing."

"And have you contacted the police?"

"A cursory search of the dock and the adjacent warehouses was made, but with no result and, I regret, no further pursuit. The police have no more concern than did Captain Parnell."

As Hong wrote, Ming continued the questioning. "Please describe the objects in the crate."

A blue porcelain urn, so high," he held his hand palm down three feet from the floor, "decorated with vines and flowers. And a . . ." He fumbled for a word. "Terracotta figure of a horse and rider, so large." He indicated the size with both hands this time.

"Were any other crates stolen from that shipment?"

"Not that I have been told, but it is possible."

"Was the crate marked in a special way that would have gotten attention?"

"Not at all. It had simple shipping information and Customs seals."

"Was the crate insured?"

"I am embarrassed to say that it was not; an oversight on the part of my cousins."

Hong resumed. "You say that the objects' monetary value is slight, yet they have been in your family for many years. Could their age give them greater value than you might think?"

Sing shook his head. "I may have exaggerated their age. Neither is a great antiquity, say as something from the Second Dynasty might be."

"Perhaps then the theft was random, a simple act of opportunity."

"That is possible, but whatever the circumstance, I must have the crate back."

Hong pushed the paper and the inkwell across the desk. "Please write down the shipping and lading information."

"Better still" said Ling, "I can give you the bill of lading. He reached into his coat pocket and pulled out a small sheaf of papers. "The Customs form is there as well." He set the papers on the desk. "Do you think you can help me?"

"That is possible," said Hong. "Let us make some inquiries. We will contact you with the result."

Ling reached into his suit coat. "What retainer do you require?"

"None yet," said Ming. "We customarily do not accept a retainer before we study a case. If it appears that we may be of service, then we can discuss terms."

Sing's smile slipped a little. "I see. How soon will I hear from you?" His submerged impatience was slowly rising to the surface.

"Our operatives will make discreet enquiries and gather information. Then we will evaluate the case. By this time tomorrow we should have a better grasp of the situation." The brothers rose. Behind Ling, the door slid back and Raphael stood in the hallway.

"Raphael will show you to the gate," said Ming.

Sing rose from his chair and hesitated as if to press the brothers further, then he wisely turned and stepped into the hall where Raphael stood with his hat and coat.

As Raphael and Ling descended the stairs, Ming took a cigarette from the jade box on the desk. He offered one to Hong and struck a match to light both. Neither spoke until they could see Raphael and Ling walking down the drive toward the gate.

"What do you think?" said Ming.

Hong let out a lungful of smoke. "I think it was clever of you to refuse his retainer in that fashion. Certain parts of his story seem suspect."

"He mentioned Captain Parnell and the police, but he made no mention of alerting Customs. Does he perhaps wish to avoid their involvement?"

"Perhaps, and if so, why?"

"When Darby returns, we should have him investigate Mister Sing before we embrace him as a client."

"I concur. We should find out what businesses he serves. I'm going to ring for Raphael. I think tea would be good right now."

"And tonight, the opera."

"Yes, the opera. The premiere of *Don Giovanni*. I can't wait to hear Maria sing Donna Elvira. She will be wonderful."

"You do the lady an injustice, brother. She will be heavenly."

"She will be a perfect Elvira, although I hope someday we might hear her sing the role of Donna Anna."

Ming and Hong had the misfortune to have fallen in love with the same woman, diva Maria Donatelli, the beautiful and extraordinarily talented soprano of San Francisco's Massimo Opera Company. The buxom, dark-haired beauty loved Ming and Hong as dearly, but knew that it would break the heart of one to choose the other and break hers in the bargain.

Ming pulled the bell cord to summon Taylor, their bodyguard and coachman. "Shall we send white roses or red?"

"For the role of Donna Elvira, definitely red."

Taylor entered shortly. If a chiffonier had arms, it would resemble Ike Taylor, almost as broad as he was tall, and as muscular as a gorilla. Rumors that his suits were sewn by a tentmaker were factually false, but in principle, close to the truth.

"Yes, sirs?"

"We will be leaving for the opera at seven o'clock," said Ming. "Please have the carriage ready."

"And please go to Peck's and order two dozen red roses to be delivered to Miss Donatelli's dressing room this evening. And tell them to have them there before curtain this time."

"And the card?" said Taylor, accustomed to the chore.

Ming turned to Hong. "With warmest regards?"

Hong laughed. "Ever the romantic. Taylor, have the card read, 'with deepest affection, Hong and Ming.'"

"Why not 'Ming and Hong'?" Ming jibed. Taylor didn't laugh, although he wanted to. He was accustomed to the brothers' rivalry.

"Very well," said Hong, "'With deepest affection, the Brothers Smith.'"

"Will there be anything else, sirs?"

"Yes, Taylor, please tell Raphael to bring us tea." He turned to Ming. "Darjeeling? Or would you prefer Oolong?"

"Definitely Darjeeling. Thank you, Taylor."

Darby returned an hour later with little to show for his effort. As he often put it, "You cast the net and sometimes you haul in the big fish with all the little ones. Other times they slip away. You just have to keep trying."

Hong picked up a white jade sphere from the desk and turned it over in his fingers. "At this point we don't know who may have hired Bailey."

"It's not exactly a narrow field of suspects," Darby said. "Half of the city is involved in something shady, and half of that half has reason to hate you."

"But someone with big money hired Bailey," said Ming.

"Unless Frisco's underworld took up a collection."

Hong laughed. "That would be enterprising of them. I'd find it flattering if it were so."

"What is the old Arab proverb? 'You shall judge a man by the quality of his enemies?'" said Ming. "I suppose quantity is as valid a standard." He took a cigar from the cut glass humidor on the end table and snipped it at its center. He handed one half to Hong and drew the other under his nose. "One benefit of owning Oriental Trading. We enjoy sampling the best of all worlds, often before anyone else. These cigars are from Cuba. Try one if you like."

Darby accepted the offer, and soon the study was wreathed in fragrant smoke. "Another matter has come up," said Hong. "We have been approached by a Mister Sing Chung to investigate a theft. Is the name familiar?"

Darby stared at the glowing tip of the cigar, thinking. "I've heard of Sing Chung, but I don't know much about him. He has a few connections at City Hall."

"Learn what you can and report to us tomorrow morning. We have to make a decision."

"Do I bring in Chang?" Chang Tzu, Darby's Chinatown counterpart was a frequent asset, a pair of slanted eyes where Caucasians like Darby were unwelcome.

"If you can find him."

"I know where to look." Darby rose and strode to the doors. He turned and said, "And thanks for the cigar. I can't remember smoking a better one."

"…we don't know who…hired Bailey."

Opera had always enjoyed the patronage and adoration of San Francisco from mid-century since the evening when the Pellegrini Opera Company first performed Bellini's *La Somnambula* and on any given evening, the city offered the choice of as many as five different performances. Tonight, however, Ming and Hong had no choice to make. The premiere of Mozart's *Don Giovanni* featuring Maria Donatelli as Donna Elvira was a must.

For the premiere, Ming and Hong dressed in white tie and tails, their clothing cleverly tailored to give the illusion at further than three feet that they were in fact two separate men standing at an oblique angle. Their vests and shirt fronts were designed to cover and all but conceal the arm-like trunk of flesh and bone that joined them at the chest.

They stood before the wide pier glass as each tied a neat bow in his tie and arranged it under the wings of his collar.

"Your tie is crooked," scolded Ming.

"Your eye is crooked," said Hong.

As the clock struck seven, Raphael brought their high silk hats, canes, and black velvet capes. Taylor was waiting below with the carriage.

"With all due respect, sirs, please be careful."

Hong raised the lower hem of his vest to reveal the handle of a small Colt pistol. "Just in case," he said with a laugh. "Although I hardly think anyone would be foolish enough to make an attempt on our lives in front of a thousand people, including the Mayor and the Chief of Police."

"If someone really wants to kill us and he can't do it at the Opera House, he'll do it while we're dining in a restaurant, or riding down the street in a carriage, or sitting on a bench in the park. Fear is the strongest cage, and we won't be prisoners."

"As you wish, sirs," Raphael said, his diffidence masking his concern.

Taylor wore the same suit he'd worn earlier that day, a double-breasted grey pinstripe cut to conceal the pair of .45 caliber revolvers he wore in a leather shoulder rig under each arm. He opened the carriage door and let down the steps. The brothers wheeled to the right and sidestepped up, Ming in the lead. They settled into the leather seat and in a moment, they were on their way to the Grand Opera House.

No city came alive at night like San Francisco. From the Battery to the Tenderloin, from the Heights to the theater district, the streets and sidewalks were thronged with people and carriages that flowed like a bustling river through the winding streets.

When the carriage stopped in front of the Grand Opera House, a red coated doorman opened the door and bowed as the brothers sidestepped onto the walk. "Good evening, gentlemen," he said as they passed him. The crowd murmured, but no one pointed or stared. San Francisco was accustomed to the Smith Brothers and their appearance. They were greeted with smiles and nods from the most respected members of society.

Hong and Ming were escorted to their box by a liveried usher, and they took their place on the red velvet settee. Below them the crowd ebbed and flowed to the lush dissonance of the tuning orchestra.

The great chandelier that hung from the ceiling sparkled from thousands of crystal teardrops, casting myriad rainbows on the vines, flowers and figures that adorned the proscenium arch like the sugar figures on an elaborate birthday cake.

Hong peered over the brass railing. "The crowd is very large. The premiere should be a sellout."

"Did you expect any less?" Ming smiled in anticipation.

The opera was a place where San Francisco's elite came to see and to be seen. Tickets were often costly and difficult to obtain, but San Franciscans paid the price gladly. It offered an opportunity for the upper reaches of society to parade in their finery and enjoy some highbrow entertainment in a refined setting. The location of one's seats in the opera house was every bit as important an indicator of status as a family crest. A box such as the one the brothers held at the Grand Opera House signified Olympian rank.

Directly across the auditorium, Mayor Arthur Collins and his wife Bertha were entering his box, the stage right counterpart of the brothers' box. Behind them came Robert Petterel, the Commissioner of Police and his fiancée Gwendolyn Myles. The Mayor raised a hand in greeting and the brothers smiled and waved back. Petterel gave a curt nod and consulted his program.

"The Commissioner still hasn't gotten over our solving the Fishbine matter ahead of his detectives," said Hong, lowering his opera glasses.

Ming snorted. "If he could keep them out of Ah Toy's, San Francisco would be a safe place for all of us."

Someone tapped at the door to the box. It opened a foot and Taylor stuck his head in. "I left the carriage at the livery on Eleventh Street. I'll be right outside if you need anything."

People who passed in the corridor saw the giant standing guard in front of the door to the box, nearly obscuring it with his bulk. He denied access to any and everyone. The Smith Brothers were not to be disturbed while Maria Donatelli was performing.

Sidelights dimmed. The orchestra stilled and so did the crowd. Maestro Giuseppe Bartolini, the conductor, climbed the stairs from beneath the stage into the pit. His tuxedoed form was capped by a swirling mane of white hair that flowed seamlessly into his long beard. He bowed to the audience in acknowledgement and nodded to the first violin. He took his place at the podium and raised his baton.

The low brass of the trombones struck the sonorous chords of the overture's andante beginning, and Bartolini's left hand rose, the fingers curling as if around the leash of a menacing beast that he alone could control. The strings crept in with their trilling four note motif, and the sound swelled to fill the auditorium.

"Glorious," said Ming, closing his eyes. And the music swept them to another world.

VI

*D*arby was never nervous entering Chinatown, unlike many of his former colleagues. "It's all a matter of knowing how to behave," he was fond of saying. "You walk in afraid of getting your throat cut, you will." He liked to think that his years of story chasing in the famous quarter had made him so familiar a face on its streets that he was no more noticed than a man with a queue, but it was more likely the fear of Chang Tzu that made Darby untouchable. Even the San Francisco Tong hesitated to attack Chang and his people, the Sons of Thunder; they stepped around each other like a pair of lions, knowing that someday the fight was inevitable and would likely destroy them all.

On Jackson Street, sidewalk merchants offered an array of nearly anything alive or dead. Baby alligators, embroidered silk, jade and ivory dragons, chickens, some plucked and some still feathered, ornate paper lanterns, lacquered vases, and clothing of every description. A bale of cotton stood beside one stall and two men in queues haggled in rapid fire Mandarin with great gesticulation over a price for it beside a grandfather clock and a terracotta dragon the size of a pony. Darby was convinced that if you asked a Chinatown merchant for a blue ostrich, and he didn't have one in his shop, he'd have one for you in a half hour. And food; the scent of dozens of woks sending their steam into the crowded street: the scents of duck, pork, and fish overlaid with the ever present odor of fried rice and cooking oil.

He turned from Jackson Street into Ross Alley, "The Street of the Gamblers" so named for the number of Mah-Jongg parlors and other gambling dens that filled its blocks. Day or night, the crush of people filled the alley coming and going, all men; no women in sight. There were no bright silks and robes here, only the dark loose clothing of laborers, coming to Ross Alley to gamble away their wages on the hope of sudden wealth.

Darby stopped at a familiar door, painted red, a sign above it showed a golden dragon. Its tail embraced a set of characters. Darby understood some spoken Mandarin but was better at reading the characters: The House of Fortune. He rapped at the door with his walking stick, a cane that concealed a two foot sword. An eye slit opened and as quickly closed and Darby heard the sound of twin bolts being thrown. The door opened and he stepped into the House of Fortune.

"Welcome, Mister Darby." The doorman bowed respectfully and Darby returned the courtesy. The wizened man wore an embroidered red silk smock and a pillbox hat. His wisps of white moustache hung to his chest. Down the narrow hallway, Darby heard the click of tiles and exclamations of triumph and despair.

"Chang Tzu?" Darby's eyebrows raised in question.

"This way," the little man said in Mandarin. As Darby followed him down the hallway, he saw the handles of a pair of razor-edged hatchets crisscrossed in his belt at the small of his back. Through a beaded curtain at the end of the hallway, he saw men at tables and in a far corner, the man he sought.

Chang Tzu was taller than most Chinese at nearly six feet, and he was as lean and hard as the handle of a buggy whip. He shunned the traditional braid down his back, and wore his hair pulled back in a jet-black ponytail. Two features distinguished his face, a star-shaped birthmark under his right eye and a livid scar from the left side of his nose to the corner of his mouth.

He looked up from the game at Darby. "What?"

"Work."

Chang turned a tile and muttered in Mandarin.

"Pung!" called a player across the table. He took the tile and matched it with two of his own.

"This is not a good time, Darby," said Chang. "I've been losing all day, and I feel my luck about to change."

"Come with me now, and you'll come back with more money to gamble away." Chang nodded and said something in Chinese beyond Darby's ken to the other three players at the table. Chang laid three coins on the table and turned all of his tiles face up. "Chum for the sharks," he said in English, putting a cap on his head.

In the alley, Darby had to step quickly to match the taller man's purposeful strides as they wove through the thickly crowded pavement. The throngs of men seemed to part before Chang as if by some instinct, while Darby had to weave his way among the crush of bodies like a fish threading through a thick bed of kelp.

Three blocks up Jackson Street, Chang stepped into the doorway of a restaurant. Its door posts were emblazoned with carved and painted characters. This was Tim Soo's. Chang led the way past the hostess and three waiters who looked through them as if they were invisible. Through a door beside the noisy kitchen, they entered a small dim room. When Darby closed the door behind him, the din from the other side fell to a whisper.

Chang sat behind a desk, actually more a table with drawers that stood on carved dragon legs ending in ball and claw feet. From a shelf behind him, he took a decanter and two glasses. He poured bourbon for them both and pushed one of the glasses to Darby.

"How much?"

"For information, the usual rate, twenty." Darby had done the dance so many times before that it had become a reflex.

"Not enough."

Darby laughed. "I haven't even said what they want to know yet."

"When Ming and Hong Smith want to know something, it's always important, and their purse is a bottomless well. Fifty."

"What difference does it make how much you're paid? You'll lose it all at the tables or the cockfights anyway."

"True," said Chang, "but it will be mine to lose—or win."

"Twenty-five."

"Forty."

"Thirty."

"Forty-five."

Darby blinked. Chang smiled, wrinkling the scar at his lip. "You should have taken forty."

"All right, forty-five." Both men raised their glasses to each other and downed the whiskey to seal the deal. Darby counted out the bills and laid them on the table. "Sing Chung," said Darby. "Tell me what you know about him."

Chang snorted. "Sing Chung is a serpent that sheds his Chinese skin to bow and scrape to the *gāobízi* then puts it on again for his own people. He rides two horses with one ass and in the end will fall between them and be trampled."

"Colorful, but not exactly useful. Please explain." Darby took out his notebook and pencil.

"Sing Chung has been at the edges of San Francisco for some time. He became prominent in Chinatown within the last few years. He says he helps people who come here to establish themselves in business, and he does act on their behalf with the City, but at a dear price. He takes a percentage of the money any of his so-called clients may earn every week as part of the payment for his services. He has friends in City Hall who can ensure that no one operating without Sing Chung's assistance will ever obtain the proper licenses and permits. Anyone who tries on his own is quickly shut down by the police at Sing Chung's insistence."

"So he's just a shakedown artist?"

"Beyond that, he is rumored to be used by the Tong at times, and he pays half of his income to them in tribute. In exchange, he operates unmolested in Chinatown."

"He is not a member of the Tong?"

"No. The Tong would not have him. He is weak willed and lacks discipline. Sing Chung is simply an opportunist who does whatever is most profitable for himself. May I ask why the Brothers are interested in him?"

"He has approached them to engage their services. A stolen crate, as I understand, is at the heart of the business."

"My advice would be to not trust the serpent even while they are looking at him."

"I'll tell them. In the meantime, could you consult your sources?" He pushed a sheet of paper across the table. "Here are the details of the theft."

Without looking at the paper, Chang Tzu said, "How much?"

Darby grinned. "Find the crate, and you'll be playing Mah Jongg for a year."

"And if I do not?"

"The brothers will still make it worth your while."

"You were wise to come to me for answers, Darby. A word to you as a friend: ask no question about Sing Chung in Chinatown. Even I cannot protect you from the blade of the Tong."

"Thanks for the warning. Will I hear from you tomorrow?"

"Before noon, whether I succeed or not." Chang picked up the decanter. "Now let us drink as friends."

VII

*B*ackstage, Tommy Lee Cooper lay prone on the catwalk over the proscenium, his arm draped over the stock of a lever action Henry rifle, the same one his father had carried as a sharpshooter at Gettysburg. Below him, Donna Elvira was singing a plaintive aria that to Tommy Lee just sounded like so much caterwauling, but he wasn't there for the performance. Forty feet away his targets sat in a box watching the opera. His instructions were clear: don't shoot until the intermission applause can cover the sound of the rifle.

He looked over his shoulder and saw the thick rope looped over a pulley and tied to sandbags on the floor below to offset his weight. Just grab the rope and jump. An alley door would be left unlocked for him to exit, and he would get away clean. He was being paid good money to kill the Smith Brothers, enough for him to live the good life for a while, and if it looked like he might get away with it, he could blackmail the man who hired him and stretch the situation for years to come.

Tommy Lee knew nothing about Mozart, opera, or *Don Giovanni*, except that he wished intermission would come soon. All that keening in some foreign language was giving him a headache. He looked again at the rope behind him and blinked. It was tied into a noose.

A figure dropped onto his back and with a fierce backhand blow drove a metal wedge into the back of his neck. When he tried to turn to face his phantom attacker, Tommy Lee found that his arms wouldn't move. Neither would his legs. He was paralyzed.

A pair of hands lifted him to his feet and dragged him down the catwalk to the waiting noose. He wanted to scream, but his lungs wouldn't cooperate. The best he could do was an anguished gurgling that was drowned by the rumble of the timpani in the pit below. The noose slipped over his head and Tommy Lee Cooper was dropped from the walk.

Even knowing death is imminent, a man clings to hope that it may be postponed. For an instant, Tommy Lee felt that hope. The sandbags, he thought, they'll slow me down. But Tommy Lee was in free fall as he passed the rigging where the other end of the rope was knotted to a cleat in the wall. He felt the sharp yank at his neck, saw a blinding flash of white light, then nothing.

One of the dressing women was passing backstage when Tommy Lee's corpse jerked to a halt in front of her. Her screams brought Maria's aria to a sudden halt. The orchestra stopped in bits and pieces, like a complex machine shutting down.

The brothers sprang from their seat as Taylor darted into the box from the hallway, a pistol in his fist. "What's happened?"

Across the auditorium, uniformed officers, the Mayor's escort, hurried His Honor, the Commissioner and their wives out of the box. The murmur of the crowd swelled to a mild roar. The audience turned this way and that as if expecting to find an answer to what was happening written on one of the walls. Bartolini stood like a man roused from slumber, disrupting a pleasant dream.

"The Mayor has the right idea," said Taylor. "Let's get you out this box."

"Take us backstage," said Ming. "We have to see that Miss Donatelli is all right."

When Taylor hesitated, Hong said, "Now."

Alvin Thompson, the theater manager had taken the stage beside one of the uniformed officers who was asking the audience to please remain calm and exit the theater in an orderly fashion. Thompson looked ill.

Despite the policeman's order, a crowd of gawkers quickly formed backstage as word spread of a dead man hanging from the rafters. Petterel was standing beside the hanged man almost face to face with him as if they were conversing. Cooper's toes dangled inches from the floor. Beside Petterel stood Sergeant Jenkins, his personal bulldog. Petterel said to one of the uniforms, "Gather the cast and crew in one place. I want a statement from every one of them."

"He ain't one of us," said a short mustachioed man in overalls and a watch cap. He pointed at the dead man. "I never seen him before." "That's right," another chimed in. "I never saw him before, neither."

"Which of you is the stage manager?" Petterel said. A lanky man in a rumpled tweed suit stepped forward. "That would be me. Harold Peterson."

"Do you know this man?"

Peterson studied the dead man's face as if he were looking at a statue or a painting in a gallery. "Nope. He's none of my crew."

Taylor shouldered a path through the onlookers and the brothers followed in his wake. They were stopped at the edge of the crowd by two uniformed policemen. Unlike the escort cops, these men were wearing hats; they were from the street outside.

"Hold it," said one of them to Taylor, then he saw the revolver and swung his nightstick. Taylor caught the weapon in his hand and twisted it from the policeman's grip, throwing the startled cop off balance and into his partner. The crowd froze including the other officers as Taylor stood with a weapon in either hand.

"Easy, Taylor," said Ming as the brothers stepped from behind their bodyguard. "Commissioner!"

Petterel eyed them coldly and said, "Let them through."

Ming and Hong stepped forward and Taylor followed.

"No great mystery for you two to solve here; a simple suicide."

From above, a voice called out, "Sir, there's a rifle up here."

Petterel's head jerked upward in surprise. He shouted up, "Come down here." Then he turned to Jenkins and said, "Go up there and bring it down."

The brothers both winced at the thought of disturbing evidence at a crime scene. The big man clambered up rungs set in the wall with unexpected agility and returned a moment later with the rifle in his hand. He dropped the last few feet to the stage. "It was lying on the catwalk."

"Has it been fired?"

Jenkins worked the Henry's lever. A shiny cartridge spun in the air and Jenkins caught it in his hand. He held the bullet between his thumb and forefinger for Petterel to see. "Not this one." He sniffed the chamber. "It hasn't been fired."

Ming and Hong had taken advantage of the distraction to sidle over to the corpse. Ming tugged at the dead man's sleeve and the body turned slowly revealing the back of the neck. The vertebrae just above his shoulders formed an ugly bulge "There," Hong said, pointing. A dark stain had spread under the skin at the base of the dead man's skull.

"Don't touch him," snapped Petterel.

Hong said, "This is no suicide, Commissioner. This man was murdered."

"Oh, really?" said Petterel with a sneer. "Before or after he hanged himself?"

"Look at his neck. Something struck him at the base of his skull, causing subdural hematoma, hence the blood under his skin. He was alive long enough to bleed."

"His neck was broken by the fall in the noose."

"Yes, but three vertebrae below his skull, near his shoulder. This man was alive when he was hanged, paralyzed or unconscious, perhaps, but alive."

Petterel was about to order his men to remove them when Mayor Collins appeared at his side. "I put the women in the carriage and sent them home." He pointed to the hanged man. "Who is he?"

"Not part of the company. We don't know yet, but we will soon enough," then almost as an afterthought. "He had a rifle."

Collins stared at the hanging corpse. "My god. Cut him down."

Petterel turned to Jenkins. "You heard the Mayor. Do it."

Jenkins took a clasp knife from his pocket and was sawing through the rope when Ming interrupted him with a question. "Sergeant, the rifle was lying on the catwalk, correct?" Jenkins shot a look to Petterel, as if to ask his permission to answer, Petterel gave a curt nod. "Yeah, that's right; on the catwalk."

"Which way was the rifle lying? The muzzle pointed? Stage left or stage right?"

"Stage what?"

"Stage left." He pointed with his outer hand.

"Stage right," said Hong, pointing in the opposite direction.

"Left," said Jenkins, but I don't see what that has to do with anything."

"Of course not," said Hong. His eyes and Ming's drifted to their box. "Mister Mayor, you can sleep well tonight. You were not the target."

Hong saw her first. Maria Donatelli, still in her costume as Donna Elvira, stood at the fringe of the crowd. The brothers went directly to her and each took one of her hands in his. "Are you all right, Maria?" said Ming.

"Yes, I am a little bit shaken. What a terrible thing to happen, for that man to kill himself."

Ming and Hong looked to each other and an unspoken thought passed between them. Better that she not know, at least not at this moment.

"And it is a shame that it interrupted your aria," said Hong, "but there will be other performances." He turned his head toward the knot of policemen, which had grown to more than a dozen as others came in from the street. "Commissioner," he said. Petterel turned toward him.

"Miss Donatelli has suffered great distress over this incident. It is obvious that she had nothing to do with this man's death, since she was on the stage singing when it occurred. May she be excused so that we might take her home?"

Petterel waved a dismissive hand. "Yes. Take her home. If we need a statement from her, we can get it tomorrow." The brothers realized Petterel's agreement was less a concern for Maria's welfare than his desire to be rid of them.

"Thank you," she said, squeezing their hands. "I'll go change. Meet me at my dressing room door in ten minutes."

Taylor threw the nightstick to the copper who'd swung it at him and grinned. The cop glared back. "Another day, friend."

Taylor's smile fell like a window shade. "Count on it." He spun on his heel to follow his bosses. "Do you want me to bring the carriage around?"

"Yes," said Ming. "Bring it to the stage door, and try to avoid irritating the police any further."

The brothers stood patiently outside Maria's dressing room as ten minutes turned to twenty.

"Two tries at us in as many days," said Ming.

"Yes. It makes me think that the attempts are pre-emptive."

"How so?"

"The nearness of the two attempts to each other suggests a sense of urgency to put us out of the way in advance of something we haven't yet seen. If the attempts were simple revenge, the people responsible would take time to regroup, realizing that we would be on our guard."

"I agree, unless, of course, the two incidents are unrelated, pure coincidence."

"And there is the matter of the police this evening; so many so quickly. Were they waiting in the wings, as it were, expecting trouble?"

"That is a question to be probed—ah! Here comes Maria."

Maria stepped out of her dressing room as if she were going to dinner at a posh restaurant. She wore a pale green dress with a modest bustle and a fur piece draped across her shoulders. She carried a small purse in one hand and in the crook of her arm she carried roses.

Taylor avoided the street in front of the opera house and threaded the carriage through a series of byways and alleys. Maria sat in the seat opposite the brothers. When they emerged onto Manson Place, the neighborhood was quiet, the city bustle far behind them.

Maria's town house was in the center of the block. A light burned in the front window. "Louisa won't expect me so soon. I hope she's not entertaining her boyfriend."

"We could ride around for another hour," Hong said with a hopeful tone in his voice.

"No," Maria shook her head. "I'm still upset by the dead man at the theater. I heard the policeman say there was a rifle. He was going to kill you two, wasn't he?"

"We don't know that," said Ming.

"I know it," she said. "Why can't you just run Oriental Trade and be content with that?" Tears rose in her dark eyes. "Why do you have to chase every criminal in San Francisco? Why do you have to put yourselves in danger?"

Hong smiled. "The mongoose is born to fight the cobra. It has no choice. We don't have to do what we do; we want to do it because we have that choice. And that makes all the difference in the world."

"You two make me crazy," Maria said, standing as Taylor let down the carriage steps. "I have nightmares about you being killed in front of me, but that's not the worst of it. The dream goes on and I have to go on living without you." She ignored Taylor's offered hand and nearly fell clambering down the steps to the sidewalk. As she ran to her door, Ming and Hong could hear her sobs.

Ming started to rise from the seat, but Hong didn't comply, holding his brother back without making a move. "Let her go, brother. She'll cry tonight and sing again tomorrow." Then his eye fell on the abandoned roses on the carriage seat. Maria's door slammed, a jarring noise on the silent street. "Taylor, please take us home."

Darby was waiting when they arrived at the mansion. He was sitting at the dining table playing Canfield Solitaire when the brothers walked in. He looked up from his cards. "You're home early."

"The show was interrupted by a murder," Ming said, as Raphael took their hats and capes. "However, Commissioner Petterel insists on calling it a suicide. What have you learned about our friend Mister Chung?"

Darby burned with curiosity, but knew that the brothers would tell him nothing until he satisfied theirs. "Sing Chung has a foot on either side of the fence. He has big friends at City Hall and the police station, but he also is under the thumb of the Tong."

"That poses as many new questions as it answers old ones." Hong reached across the table and picked up one of Darby's cards. "Seven of diamonds on the eight of spades." He dropped the card in place.

"What was really in the crate, and does it belong to the Tong?"

"A valid question," said Hong. "Sing says that the crate was stolen, and perhaps that is correct, but if something in the crate belonged to the Tong, their resources are far better in Chinatown than our own. I should think

"Ming and Hong could hear her sobs."

they would want to find it themselves through their own devices and not involve outsiders."

"But," Ming said, "what if the Tong does not know yet? What if Sing were responsible for the delivery and has not yet told them it has gone missing?"

"Then he would seek help from such as we to find it and repair the situation before the Tong knows what has happened."

"But the next question is: who stole the crate from the dock? Was it a random act by local thieves, or was it an orchestrated scheme run by the Tong's enemies?"

Darby spoke up. "Could it have been done by Chang's men? His gang and the Tong are always jockeying for the head chair in Chinatown."

"You told him about the crate?" Ming said, pulling the bell cord to summon Raphael.

"Yeah, I did. He wanted to know why you were interested in Sing Chung. I told him about the crate, and he said he'd look into it."

Ming turned to Hong. "Do you think Chang would be disloyal to us?"

Hong laughed. "Chang is loyal only to Chang. And if he thought the crate would damage the Tong, he'd tear Chinatown apart with his bare hands to find it."

"So the question becomes, how do we manage this situation to our best advantage?"

Raphael appeared behind Darby. "What may I do for you, sirs?"

"Please make us a pot of coffee, Raphael. I expect we'll all be awake for quite a while."

The next morning, a visitor complicated matters further.

The gate bell rang at a few minutes after ten, and as the brothers watched, Raphael escorted a small man in a long, dark coat up the driveway. He was hatless, and his hair hung in long white wisps to his shoulders. As he came closer, his age became apparent; fine lines etched his face like the crazed lacquer on an old violin. His eyes betrayed his origin, a full-born Oriental, and as the brothers watched, those eyes raised to the window where they stood as if an arrow pointed at them.

"Mister Meyung Loo," said Raphael, stepping aside for the visitor to enter.

The little man radiated a calm self-possession and dignity that made Ming think of a firmly rooted oak and Hong think of a house on a stone foundation. Raphael took his coat, and under it, Meyung wore the dark pajama-like clothing of a laborer.

"Please, sit down," said Ming, surprised at the deference Meyung's demeanor inspired. "May we offer you something? Tea, perhaps, or coffee."

Meyung sat, and his posture made him seem almost as tall in the chair as he was when he stood. He sat perfectly still, except for his eyes, which studied the brothers from their heads to their boots. Ming and Hong were accustomed to the stares of the curious, but there was no curiosity in Meyung's piercing gaze. They were being weighed and measured.

Finally, Meyung spoke. "I have come a great distance on a mission of utmost importance. I apologize for my speech, but I only recently learned to speak English when I learned that I must come here."

"Your English is fine, sir," said Hong, "but if it would make you more comfortable, we can converse in Mandarin."

"My comfort is of no consequence. I will get to the point." He stood and pulled the sleeves of his loose black shirt to the elbows. The underside of each forearm was tattooed; the left with a seven-pointed star, an eye at its center, the right arm with a three-headed dragon, its tail wrapped around three rhombi. "Do you know these symbols?" said Meyung.

Both brothers shook their heads.

"I am a priest of the temple of Quang-Chi in the mountains of the land you would call Xinjiang."

"The 'new frontier,'" said Ming, "liberated from the Tajik conquerors twenty years ago."

"Yes. My brothers and I have come to San Francisco in search of something stolen from our monastery, the Eye of Quang-Chi. I understand that you men find the lost and the stolen. We want you to find the Eye."

Ming drew a sheet of paper from the desk and picked up a pen. "Please describe it." When Meyung's brow furrowed, Ming repeated the request in Mandarin.

"Yes, describe. The eye of Quang-Chi is a red jewel, what you would call a ruby. For centuries, it has rested in the head of the statue of Quang-Chi in our temple. At the creation of the world, it is said that Quang-Chi traded one of his eyes to Pan-Gu in exchange for true vision, which made him a god. His statue had one empty eye and one filled by the red jewel.

In times of trouble, we pray to Quang-Chi, and the eye weeps red tears to remove our sin. Then life becomes good once again.

"Now, both eyes are empty, for three of your months past; someone stole the jewel."

"How large is the jewel?" said Hong.

"The size of a duck's egg. and as clear as mountain water. But this is no simple theft. The thief's motive may have been greed, but those who enlisted him have darker designs."

"Please explain."

"The Emperor would have all of us worship him, the better to force his will on us all. To take the eye of Quang-Chi is to render our order powerless in the eyes of our people. Without the anchor of a benign god to give them the will to resist, they will fall under the emperor's yoke."

He paused and Hong asked, "You believe that the theft of the eye was a political act?"

Meyung pondered the question. "Yes. And the minions of the emperor enlisted criminals to smuggle the Eye out of China."

"You speak of the Tong," said Ming, a statement, not a question.

The calm of Meyung's face melted, replaced by a look of fierce rage. "Yes the Tong. Animals, they would sell their own mothers for gold and power," he hissed. Meyung took a deep breath. "My apologies. At times my emotions are hard to control."

"But the Tong did not steal the jewel?" said Hong.

"No, I am ashamed to say. The thief was one of our own brotherhood; a novice monk seduced by greed."

"And has he been found?"

Meyung nodded. "And punished for his crime. But before he died, he told us of the plan to take the jewel to America."

"Why not have it cut and sell it in pieces or put it into jewelry?"

"Because the emperor wants it whole once he has — "a pause — "subdued our people, put them under his heel. He can display the Eye as a justification of his actions, a symbol of his power. If we can restore the Eye, our people will have the hope to resist him once again."

"I do not understand," said Ming. "The Emperor has such great resources at his disposal. Why would he send the jewel to America when he could hide it in his own land?"

"The situation is more delicate than I can convey. We are one — what is your word for the spotted tiles?"

"Domino?"

"Yes, we are but one domino in a line poised to fall one after the other. Should the jewel be found anywhere in China and be traced to the Emperor, the response would be immediate and severe."

Hong said, "You mentioned brothers. How many have come with you in search of the jewel?"

"Five of my order have come with me. Together, we hoped to recover the Eye and return it to our monastery, but once we arrived here, we realized that we cannot do so alone. This is why I come to you."

"Sir," said Ming, "How long have you been in San Francisco?"

"Six days."

"And in that time, have you tried to trace the jewel on your own?"

"We have tried, but we find our path blocked at every turn by fear of the Tong and fear of your police. Someone may know something of the Eye but fears to say."

"We can make enquiries," said Ming, but we cannot guarantee success."

"I understand, but you will help us search for the Eye?"

"As my brother said, we can make enquiries."

"Of course you shall be paid for your services." Meyung drew a small pouch from beneath his shirt and poured its contents onto the desk, forming a cone of golden dust. "Is this enough?"

"Perhaps you should keep your gold until we are sure we can help you."

"I am sure," said Meyung. "Or Quang-Chi would not have sent me to you. And he will protect you as you make your search."

"Protect us?"

"There are already people who wish you dead. Soon there will be more."

IX

"**We** are faced with a dilemma." Ming poured tea from the silver pot on the desk. He and Hong stared at the mound of gold dust still on their desk. Meyung Loo had refused to take it with him when he left, insisting that the brothers were now in his employ.

"I agree," said Hong. "In taking up the cause of the Quang-Chi order, we set ourselves in opposition to the Tong, with whom Sing Chung is allied. It creates an oblique conflict of interest."

"Are you are thinking as I do that these two matters may be intertwined?"

"That is possible," said Hong. "If Sing's stolen crate contains the Eye of Quang-Chi, it is an odd coincidence that both ends of the rope should meet at our door."

"And if they are connected, it may be useful to stay with both for a time to see where the knot may be tied."

"So long as it is not around our throats."

"Are you thinking that the attempts on our life are related as well?"

"People have tried before, but never with such urgency. Yet, if the Tong were connected to the attempts, I would expect them to use their own people, not Americans."

"I agree, that is puzzling. If not the Tong, then who?"

"I hope we find out soon enough."

A knock sounded at the door and Darby came in. "It cost a few bucks, but I found out who the shooter was: a boy from Pennsylvania, Tommy Lee Cooper. He had a thousand bucks in cash in his pocket, but not much else."

"And Petterel?" said Ming.

"He's holding to the official story that Cooper was hired to kill Mayor Collins. At least that's what he told the reporters this morning. It'll hit the afternoon papers." He noticed the mound of gold dust on the desk and whistled. "Did you two strike it rich?"

"A retainer from a new client," said Ming."Have you heard from Chang yet?"

"No, but I should shortly. He said by noon, but to Chang, time is flexible."

"I'm curious what he may have uncovered about the mysterious crate," said Hong.

"If it's in Chinatown, Chang will find it," Darby paused, "if the Tong don't have it already."

"If the Tong had the crate, I suspect Sing Chung would not be seeking our services."

"What are you going to do about him?"

"We were just discussing that issue. Something new has emerged, a perhaps related matter."

Ming went on to tell of Meyung Loo's visit and his order's quest for the Eye of Quang-Chi. "There are wheels within wheels in operation," he said. "Nothing is as it appears on the surface."

"If Sing Chung is responsible for the jewel and it has slipped his grasp, he must be desperate to get it back before his masters find out."

"Maybe the Tong have got it and they're running their own game separate from the emperor. Maybe they're holding out for the highest bidder," Darby said.

"If they have the Eye. We can't be sure that they do."

Hong added, "No, we can't, but until we know for certain, we have to act as if it were still in play. That's the only way we can hope to find it."

"And if the Tong don't have it, then who does?"

Ming stared at the gold on the desk. "Someone we have yet to see."

Raphael came in. "Sirs, there is a man outside the gate."

"I didn't hear the bell," said Ming.

"He hasn't rung, sirs. He is simply standing outside ten feet away, hidden from the street in the bushes but you can see him from the inside. He is simply standing; he hasn't moved for some time."

Ming and Hong rose from the desk and walked to the window. Hong held a pair of binoculars to his eyes for a moment then handed them to Ming. Ming looked through them for a moment then passed the glasses to Darby.

In the shrubbery outside the estate, a man stood in a posture that would be interpreted as attention in a soldier if his arms were not folded, his right hand inside his left sleeve.

"He wears no queue. He is dressed in exactly the same clothing as Meyung. I'd say the man is a member of the Quang-Chi order."

Hong nodded. "My thoughts exactly."

"I'd bet he's got his hand on a weapon up his sleeve. Is this what Meyung meant when he said we would be 'protected'?"

"And if so, were we under that protection at the opera?"

"Holy Moses," said Darby. "You mean one of those monks killed Cooper? If that's the case, how did they know you'd be there, and he'd be there, and that he was going to kill you?"

"We certainly did not tell them," said Hong. "Apparently we are being watched by many pairs of eyes."

Ming added, "And stalked by many pairs of feet."

*C*hang walked all the way around Sun Yo's chair without speaking. Sun was terrified, tied blindfolded to his seat. The shopkeeper's skinny knees trembled as he heard the footsteps circle his chair. An hour ago three strangers had come into the shop where he sold artworks, painted screens, vases and urns, carved jade and ivory.

Without a word they had seized him, dragged him to the back room of the shop and tied his wrists to the arms of the chair and his ankles to its legs. He was gagged and blindfolded with silk scarves from a counter display and the men left. He heard the tinkle of the spring bell over the front door and heard it slam, then silence.

Who were these men? What had he done? And the greatest question: what would happen next?

Sun Yo was a fence. In the front of his shop he sold pedestrian items. Through his back door, he trafficked in stolen goods, particularly in jade, but like all the merchants on his street, he paid tribute to the Tong every week for their protection. He had paid them just four days ago. What had he done? Whom had he offended?

After trying his bonds, he realized that he could not escape the expert knots. As he sat in the chair, sightless, his hearing became more acute. He could hear the scratching of a rat in the walls, the muffled shout of an angry man in the street, and from the alley behind, the soft strains of a flute.

When the door bell rang again, it seemed as loud as the chime of the Custom House clock. The door closed. No one called his name or asked where he was. The visitor knew. Footfalls crossed the floor and came behind the counter. Sun's teeth would have chattered were the scarf not tied so tight. The footsteps circled the chair and stopped in front of him.

Sun felt the cold steel of a knife slip under the scarf beside his eye. A quavering moan escaped his throat. Then with a flick of the blade, the scarf fell away. Sun found himself staring into Chang Tzu's scarred face.

"You know who I am?" Chang said in Mandarin.

Sun's head bobbed spasmodically, his eyes wide.

"Then you know that I will kill you without a thought." He slipped the knife under the gag. "This blade will cut either way. Cry out and you die."

Sun stared downward at the knife hand, almost out of his line of sight. A sharp hiss, and the silk fell away from his mouth, but Sun was too shocked to close it. Chang held the blade an inch from Sun's eye. He could see the flickering light of a candle gleaming on the polished steel.

"Two days ago, a crate was stolen from the wharf, a crate from the Parma Queen. It held statuary, a mounted horseman and a painted vase. What do you know about this?"

Sun's jaw trembled. "I-I-I know nothing."

"None of your harbor rats has come slinking down your alley with it?"

"No, I swear it. No one has come to me with such things as you describe. No one."

"You are one with the Tong. Have they sworn you to silence?"

Sun shook his head side to side, on the verge of hysteria. "No. No. No one but you has spoken of this."

Chang brought the tip of the knife to the corner of Sun's mouth. He drew the razor-edged blade across the flesh and a small runnel of blood trickled down Sun's chin and dripped a red spot onto his starched collar. "Hear me, Sun Yo: if I discover that you have deceived me, I will cut out your lying tongue and nail it between your eyes. And if you tell anyone that I have been here or what I seek, I will take those eyes first."

The words tumbled from Sun's mouth like coal from a spilled scuttle. "No. No one. I will tell no one."

The three men who had lashed Sun to the chair came in and stood behind Chang. "Untie him," As they did, Chang crouched, putting himself at eye level with Sun. "Look at me, Sun Yo. If you hear any word about the crate, you will tell me and no one else. You pay the Tong to protect you, but remember this. I put you at my mercy this day. I can do so again at my will." Chang reached into his pocket and took out a five dollar gold piece. He pushed it between Sun's lips. "For your trouble." Chang spun on his heel and left, his men in his wake.

Sun sat frozen to the chair and wept unashamedly at his close brush with Death.

On the street, Chang cursed in frustration. He had grilled his best sources in Chinatown and knew no more about the crate than he did when he began. If he could find the crate before the Smith Brothers, he could deal directly with Sing Chung and likely extract a good price for it. And if its contents were tied in some way to the Tong, it could prove invaluable to him in the struggle for power in Chinatown.

The next person he must ask is Sing Chung himself, but that approach must be made with caution. Sing was under the Tong's direct protection and was no simple merchant. He had powerful friends in City Hall as well as Chinatown, and to touch him was to touch the Tong's eyeball. I must plan and wait for my chance, Chang thought. In the meantime, I will meet with Darby. I have nothing to tell him, but he may have more to tell me than he has already.

XI

Raphael was clearing the dishes from lunch and the brothers were enjoying coffee when the gate bell rang. "I shall see who that is, sirs. Are you disposed to receive visitors?"

"Yes, Raphael," said Ming. "But first, please look to the gate and see who it might be."

Raphael disappeared for a moment then returned to say. "Sirs, Mister Sing is at the gate. Shall I admit him?"

"Of course," said Hong. "We will meet with him in our office."

Raphael nodded his acknowledgement and backed out of the room.

"Shall you give him the bad news or shall I?" said Hong.

"You are more diplomatic, brother. Be my guest."

They took their seat behind the desk. Hong wet his index finger on the tip of his tongue and touched a spot on the desk where the mound of gold dust has rested the day before. He held his finger under the lamp and smiled at the few bright flecks that sparkled in the light. "Meyung Loo's gold is considerable."

"But I fear that its obligation may prove a heavy yoke."

At the sound of footfalls on the stair, the conversation ceased. When Sing Chung sat across the desk from Ming and Hong, he looked haggard. His eyes were red from lack of sleep, and his meticulous appearance had slipped considerably. He was unshaven, and his collar was askew, his ascot loose around his throat.

"Have you learned anything about my crate?"

"I regret that we are unable to help you, sir," said Hong. "Our resources have uncovered no information. The trail seems to have gone cold. Had you come to us sooner…"

"Can't you keep looking?" Sing burst out. "I'll pay whatever you ask. You must keep looking!"

"Sir, we cannot in good conscience take your money if we cannot produce results."

Sing's eyes twitched back and forth then bored into Hong. "They've gotten to you, haven't they? Or did you go to them behind my back? You half-breed bastards…"

He leapt from the chair and as quickly was seized by the shoulders and slammed back into the seat by Raphael. The butler's hands slid down

Sing's arms and closed in a painful twisting grip on his triceps. Sing's face contorted in pain. Raphael pulled Sing from the chair and raised him onto the toes of his high-button shoes. "This way, sir," said Raphael, in the same measured tones he used all day, as he steered Sing through the doorway and into the hall.

"I'll get you for this," bellowed Sing. "I have resources too. You treacherous dogs!" His ranting disappeared down the stairs and in a moment, the brothers saw Raphael walking Sing to the gate, Sing's hat on his head and his coat over one arm.

"Your choice of words last night – desperate?"

"Yes," said Hong. "It seems we are correct. He is desperate to find the crate, and for reasons other than family honor."

"But we will continue to search for it." A statement, not a question.

"Indeed. We simply will do so without obligation to Sing Chung. Should we find the crate, we will then decide where our obligations may lie and act as we see fit."

"Sing said 'they' as if we should know who they may be."

"Perhaps the Tong," said Hong.

"I don't think so," said Ming, tapping the stub of a pencil in the palm of his hand. "If the Tong came to us, he would know already."

"Unless the Tong stole the crate and do not want him to know that they do. As you said, brother, wheels within wheels."

"When we find the crate, all questions will be answered."

"When? You're being optimistic today."

"When do we fail?"

"What business do you have with that man?" The brothers looked up startled at the voice. Meyung Loo stood in the doorway. His wrinkled face was twisted into a look of fury. "Answer me!" He stormed into the room. In seconds, Raphael came up silently behind him, cocking a pistol pointed at his skull. Ming read the question in the butler's eyes.

Ming put both hands palms out. "Hold." Raphael froze but did not relax his stance. The priest snarled, ignoring his peril.

"Meyung, our respect goes only so far," said Hong in Mandarin. "Perhaps in your temple, you are the absolute authority, but this is not Xinjiang. Your behavior is unacceptable, even for a client."

"That man is a thief, a liar, and he is in league with the Tong." Meyung spat the last word as if it were a curse. "And you counsel with him as you would with me?"

"Because we respect you, I will answer your question – this one time, but never again will we permit you to challenge our methods or interrupt our work." He took the pouch with Meyung's gold from a drawer in the desk. He poured it out. "There is your gold. Take it back if you wish, and go to someone else for help. But if you want us to aid you, remember your place."

Meyung glared but did not speak, nor did his hand move toward the gold.

"If you saw Sing Chung enter our house, you also saw him leave. Perhaps you noticed the difference between Raphael's behavior toward him coming and going. We did not part on friendly terms. If we are to help you, we will speak with many people, some perhaps your enemies and some whom you consider the scum of the earth, but each has his use to us. Do we understand each other?"

Meyung's eyes glared his answer.

"Raphael will show you out," said Hong, switching to English. "The next time you come, please ring the bell."

Both brothers busied themselves with papers on their desk until they heard the closing of the downstairs door.

"As you said last night about being watched," Hong said, taking a cigarette from the case. He offered one to Ming, who shook his head."I don't mind that so much as Meyung getting past Raphael to get in here."

"To be fair, Raphael was giving the bum's rush to Sing Chung."

"Maybe we should post guards 'til this business is over."

"Not a bad idea. We can have Tom and Orville stay on the property and they can trade off shifts." Tom Hunt and Orville Hankins were a pair of former Pinkerton agents whose penchant for brutality exceeded even the Pinkertons' reputation. They were happy to be larger fish in a bigger bowl than the Agency would allow. They found San Francisco to their taste as a city and the Smith Brothers to their taste as employers.

"Yes, Orville and Tom will do, and we can still take Taylor with us when we go out."

"Seems the most sensible course." Ming reached for the bell pull.

XII

*D*arby never liked waiting, although working for the brothers had taught him its necessity. "Sometimes," as Hong said, "you must sit very still for a long time if you want to catch the big fish." Darby was waiting now at a table in the back of Tim Soo's, the last of his moo goo gai pan going cold on the plate. He had read the *Times* through and drunk two pots of tea. He wanted a beer, but he couldn't risk it. He'd likely need a clear head once Chang reported to him.

Chang had said by noon, but it was now after two and still no sign of the man. Darby wanted to get up and go out into the street to start looking for him but knew better. Chang would come when he was ready, and not one second sooner. The restaurant was almost empty now, ten or twelve patrons at the front, when four men came in with no interest in lunch.

They were Chinese, but dressed in Western clothing, collared shirts, vests, and trousers under long coats. Their leader, a short man with a drooping moustache, scanned the room. The diners froze; food halfway to their mouths. Through the beaded curtain that divided the front half of the restaurant from the back, the leader spotted Darby. He pointed and barked an order in Mandarin. Bailey's Chinese was good enough to recognize the words, "Take him." His three companions strode to the rear, not running, but walking with unmistakable purpose. The other patrons, sensing danger, leaped to their feet and ran out the door.

Under the table, Darby pulled out the two-shot Derringer he carried in his boot. Two shots, three men. The folly of bringing a knife to a gun fight flashed through his mind. Next time he'd bring a revolver. The men were within five feet of Darby's table and one of them was reaching for a pistol under his coat when the kitchen door burst open and the cook armed with a cleaver and Tim Soo with a long chopping knife burst into the room.

Darby had seen enough street brawls in his day to be something of an expert, but he'd never seen a fight so efficiently vicious as the one before him now. It was as if five dust devils with fists and feet swirled around, the room, upsetting chairs and tables.

Darby jumped to his feet and backed into a corner, the Derringer clutched in his fist. His only escape, the kitchen, was blocked by the fight, and beside him, the door to Chang's office was locked.

Tim Soo slashed and parried, making the knife a lethal extension of his arm. He caught one of the thugs across his forehead with the tip of the blade, a tactical move to blind him with his blood. Another of the attackers charged him from behind but fell with the cleaver buried in his skull. The third man's pistol boomed and the cook's face disappeared from a shot to the back of his head.

Darby raised the Derringer and convulsively jerked the trigger, firing one barrel then the other. One shot missed, and one shot found its target. The pistol man clutched at his stomach and staggered forward but found his revolver too heavy to lift. It roared again and blew a hole through the floorboards as he fell and lay still. Tim Soo had the last of the three on the floor and was about to deliver a *coup de grâce* when a voice called out. "Stop. I want him alive."

Darby's head jerked toward the entrance and saw Chang. The short man with the moustache was gone.

"Glad you could make it." Darby laughed nervously. "I tried to hold 'em for you, but they just wouldn't wait. Who the hell are those guys? Are they Tong?"

Without a word, Chang pulled his knife and went from one of the corpses to the other, slashing their sleeves open to reveal their forearms. He put his foot on the chest of the third man, still held at bay by Tim Soo's knife. He ripped away the sleeve and stared at the man's forearm.

Over his shoulder, Chang said in English. "They are not Tong. They do not have the mark."

"Okay, I'll ask again, who the hell are those guys?"

"I do not know," said Chang, "but before the sun sets, this man will tell me."

Two of Chang's men began to lift the captive and he lashed out with his foot, catching one of the pair in the chest and hurtling him backward. He twisted free, his fingers digging in his pocket. Chang brought the butt of his knife down on the thug's head, his eyes rolled back, and he lay still.

Chang pulled the hand from the pocket. In it was a crumbling white pill. Chang sniffed at it. "Nightshade." He took a vase with flowers from the nearest table and poured the water over the attacker's hand.

"What are you doing?" Darby asked.

"I don't want him licking his fingers before I'm through with him." Then to his men, "Take him to the kitchen and bind him."

"What about the cops?" said Darby, looking toward the door. "Won't they be here soon?"

Chang smiled without mirth. "The police care little about what happens here. I pay them to look away. And as far as they are concerned, a few Chinamen, more or fewer, mean little in the great picture."

Tim Soo stared down at the dead cook. "Chu was a good cook and a loyal man."

Chang pulled a small pouch from his vest. Darby heard the clink of coins. "Give this to his family. Tell them he died honorably." Tim Soo

"Chang brought the butt of his knife down..."

nodded and set about righting the chairs and tables upset in the fight.

From the kitchen, Darby heard a scream. "Ah," said Chang. Our friend is awake. I have a few things to tell you, but if you will be patient for a short time, I may have much more. I would suggest, however, that you wait out here. You may find my methods, shall we say, unpleasant."

Darby sat at a table near the front door. The next time he heard a scream from the kitchen, he decided to have that beer after all.

XIII

*D*arby returned to the mansion just after supper to find the brothers in the parlor sitting at a backgammon board. Hong was rattling his dice in a cup.

"Backgammon?" Darby said, flopping, exhausted, into a leather wing chair. "I thought a pair of thinkers like you two would play chess."

"We used to," said Hong, spilling his dice onto the board. "He moved his pieces deliberately, the ivory pips clacking on the inlaid board, "but because we were both taught chess by Uncle Robert, our approaches and strategies are so similar that each of us may as well be playing against himself."

Ming rattled his dice. "Did you know, Darby, that all possible combinations of dice throws and move options in the first turn for each player allows a total of more than eight million possibilities? It is unlikely that Hong and I will ever duplicate a game, and the chance factor of the dice teaches one to deal with unforeseen contingencies." He threw his dice on the board and Hong groaned. "As I said." Ming moved his jade pips and put two of Hong's on the bar. "You read the *Times* today?"

"Yeah, the opera incident made the front page, but the story didn't square with everything you told me last night. That Simmons is on Petterel's leash and writes up the cop version of it all."

"No surprises there. So what have you learned from Chang?"

"That there are more players at the table than we imagined." Darby briefly recounted the battle at Tim Soo's, the questioning of the captive, and the short man with the moustache.

"Neither Chang nor Tim Soo knew this man?" said Hong.

Darby shook his head. "He was a stranger to everybody. The best that Chang could get out of the man we caught was the name Ching. He was pretty tough. He held up under Chang's torture for quite a while, but he probably would have said Confucius or Abe Lincoln in another five minutes."

"And they were not Tong?"

"Definitely not Tong. None of them was tattooed like the Tong members here. In fact none of them were tattooed at all."

"Not Tong," said Ming, "or the other gangs of Chinatown. Darby, do you recall the man standing by the gate today?"

"Yeah. What about him?"

"He was not one of these men?"

"Nope. He wasn't dressed like them either. These guys wore western clothing."

"Not Tong, not Quang-Chi," mused Hong.

"Do you think Darby's enquiries have struck a hornet's nest?"

"I do not know," said Hong, "but I don't think you should go to your flat tonight. You are welcome to stay here, Darby. We'll ring for Raphael to prepare a room for you."

"Here in the mansion?"

"Yes, Tom and Orville are bunking with Taylor in the carriage house and taking turns as watchmen."

"Well, thanks. That sounds like a good idea. By the way, do you have any more of those Cuban cigars?"

Feng Tao looked around the circle of faces at the table. The air in the basement room, little more than a dirt-floored excavation under a dry goods shop was close and foul. One of the men had lit a stick of incense and its cloying scent mixed with the smell of earth, mold, and mildew. "We failed today, and we must not fail the Emperor again, or the consequences will be dire."

"We lost three of our number," said a lean man with a thick queue. "Perhaps trying to take the American in a public place was an error."

"Not in a public place," said another. "A public place under the hand of Chang-Tzu."

"That," said Ching, "was an error, I admit, but it is one we will not make again. I believed the Tong controlled Chinatown absolutely, but that estimation of their grasp gives them too much credit. Chang Tzu's warriors do not wear a uniform; they wear the garb of everyday people and hide in plain sight in places we see without looking. That is their stealth and their strength. They are a knife up the sleeve."

"Why not just have the Tong handle matters?" said long queue. "They surely could have told us that Tim Soo's restaurant was the wrong place for such action. For that matter, why not just have them abduct this Darby for us?"

"Because we cannot trust them. At the first sign of advantage they may abandon us and seek their own gain. We trusted them to deliver the Eye, and their operative has not yet done so. Or has he? Perhaps the Tong are holding it at this moment and biding their time, hoping to ransom the Eye for greater gain to us or," he paused, "to them."

"Where else can we turn?"

For the first time since they had sat at the table, Feng Tao smiled. "It is time to tug at the leash of another of our dogs and bring him to heel."

XVI

*T*he next morning, a pair of uniforms rang the gate bell. From their window, the brothers saw Sergeant Hawkins and another officer they recognized from the opera house, waiting. Raphael went to the gate, spoke to them, and looked up to the window. Hong signaled with his hand, and Raphael opened the gate for them. The three walked up the drive and as they passed an ornate hedge, Orville stepped from behind it unseen, a lever action Winchester at port arms. He followed them with his eyes until they disappeared through the front doors.

"Wait here a moment, please," Raphael said. As he turned, the brass elevator descended with Hong and Ming inside. Hawkins half whispered a remark about monkeys in a cage and his companion snickered, until Raphael turned a baleful eye on them both.

"Good morning, Sergeant Hawkins," said Hong as they stepped from the elevator. "I am afraid I do not know your friend."

"Officer Henry Roebuck," the companion said, keeping his hands clasped behind his back as if to avoid shaking hands with the freaks.

"How do you do," said Ming. "And what may we do for you gentlemen?"

"The Commissioner wants to talk to you in his office. Now."

The brothers looked to each other and nodded. "Of course. We'll be happy to oblige." Ming turned to Raphael. "Please have Taylor bring the carriage around."

"Yes, sirs." Raphael disappeared silently down the corridor.

"May I ask what this is about?" said Hong.

"If I knowed, you'd be talkin' to me," said Hawkins.

"Very well. Did you gentlemen come in your own carriage?"

Hawkins looked at his shoes. "No, we rode a streetcar."

"Then please ride with us to City Hall."

Neither Hawkins nor Roebuck spoke during the trip uptown. Roebuck stared at Ming and Hawkins stared at Hong as if they had each been assigned to watch one brother, lest he break free and bolt from the carriage. Taylor watched the policemen over his shoulder, and Ming and Hong amused themselves with the people on the sidewalk.

The carriage pulled up at the entrance of City Hall and Taylor jumped down to lower the steps. The policemen got off first then Ming and Hong descended in their sideways fashion.

"Where will I find you inside?" Taylor said.

Hawkins quickly said, "You'll stay out here with the animals, boyo."

Taylor set his jaw and stared down the sergeant.

"It's all right, Taylor," said Ming. "Please wait with the carriage."

Taylor stepped back to allow the brothers to pass but waited until they were in the building before he climbed back into the driver's seat to move the carriage.

The brothers paused at the impossibly tall bronze-leaved doors and looked up to their full height. "What giants must pass through these portals," Hong said with a laugh.

Ming said, "Nonsense. It's tradition. They're made that way to make everyday people such as we feel insignificant."

"We'll see how well it works."

Petterel's office was on the second floor with high windows overlooking the bustling street below. Hawkins led them through an anteroom with a pretty red-haired young woman at a desk and rapped on a polished oaken door. Without waiting, he ushered the twins inside and closed the door behind him.

Commissioner Petterel sat behind a desk large enough to serve eight at dinner. He was not alone. A stout Oriental gentleman in morning coat and striped trousers sat in a nearby armchair. He balanced a high silk top hat on his knee like a circus trick while he kept his gloved hands clasped on the golden head of his cane.

Petterel didn't rise from his chair, nor did his guest. "Gentlemen," he said. "Thank you for your cooperation."

"Good morning, Commissioner," said Ming as both brothers nodded respectfully.

"I would ask you to sit, but I don't have a suitable chair. This gentleman is Sen Ti. He is from the Chinese Mission." After a suitable pause to allow the information to sink in, Petterel continued. "He has come to me with concerns about a client you have taken on."

"We have many clients," said Ming. "Perhaps you could tell us which one is such a worry."

"Don't be coy with me," Petterel hissed. "You know damned well which client, Meyung Loo. What has he hired you to do?"

Hong said, "As in the past, so today, that information is privileged for the protection of our client. We cannot divulge such facts. I suspect that since you know that he is our client and that we are in the presence of the Emperor's representative, that you already know the task at hand."

"Meyung Loo is a criminal," said Sen Ti in an oily voice. "A political radical; he and his henchmen wish to overthrow the Emperor. I can only assume that what he does in America is what he has done in my homeland, mischief."

"From a tiny corner of a mountaintop in Xinjiang? If I were the Emperor, I too would quake with fear at a handful of unarmed priests." Hong smiled.

Sen Ti's jaw set and he said through his teeth, "They defy the Emperor and their people rally behind them."

"They are no more likely to rise up and attack than a handful of ants. Or are they simply the first ants tunneling under the great tree? Does the Emperor fear that if enough ants burrow around its roots that it will topple?"

Sen Ti smiled. "You enjoy a lucrative business with my country, your Oriental Trade Consortium. You do so at my Emperor's whim. At any time, the winds may blow your ships a different way."

"If so, my brother and I could be bankrupt and penniless," Hong acknowledged, "in forty years."

"Enough. There's no argument here," Petterel snapped. "The men you represent are undesirables, and if you persist in acting on their behalf, you will share in their consequences. Consider yourselves warned."

"Duly noted," said Ming. "Before we leave, one question: how soon will the Grand Opera House reopen to resume *Don Giovanni*?"

Petterel seemed dangerous close to exploding. "When we have finished our investigation," he said through clenched teeth."

"I feared that was the case. Perhaps next season." The brothers wheeled and headed toward the door, but Hawkins blocked their way.

"You two think you're too clever to be touched, but this is no blackmailed philanderer or petty crook you're dealing with now," said Petterel. I'm prepared to bring the full weight of the department down on you."

Hong looked pointedly at the ambassador then at Petterel. "Are we perhaps the ants at the root of your tree, Petterel?"

Petterel glared at them then waved a hand for Hawkins to step aside. The sergeant opened the door and saw them out.

The ambassador had not moved since the brothers had entered Petterel's office. "Those two are dangerous." He took one hand from his cane and pointed a finger at the Commissioner. "You must deal with them."

Petterel nodded. "It's already in the works."

"See that it is done." He stood and put on his hat in one fluid motion and walked out of the office leaving Petterel staring at his back.

In the carriage, Ming and Hong were silent for a moment. Then Hong said, "That was interesting."

"Yes," said Ming, "and it reinforces my belief that Sing's missing crate and Meyung's missing jewel are of a piece."

"The cases are converging," Hong agreed.

"And Darby; was he attacked because he asked the wrong questions, or simply because he works for us? What did you make of Petterel's warning?"

"Call it what it was, a threat. Sobering."

"I agree." Hong looked at his watch. "It's almost noon. Where should we have lunch?"

"McClanahan's?"

"McClanahan's it is." Hong called up to Taylor and he wheeled the carriage east on Fourteenth Street. McClanahan's was a restaurant that catered to the art and theater crowd and their hangers-on. The building was a mansion from the gold rush days that had once been Madam McClanahan's, the most prominent brothel in the city. It is rumored that James Hampstead, who bought the building when Madam McClanahan died, found a secret compartment in a wall upstairs and behind it was a small box with the Madam's customer names on file cards. Hampstead was gentleman enough to destroy the file, to the irritation of some local and state politicians, and the great relief of others.

The ground floor held the main dining room in the former parlor, a high-ceilinged room with walnut wainscoting, stamped tin ceilings, and the original crystal chandelier imported from Paris.

The front was crowded, but Alvin, the *maitre d'* waved the twins back to a curtained booth in a room to the rear. Every eye in the restaurant followed them, but they had long since become accustomed to being a curiosity and later, celebrities. As they passed a table, Ming noticed a grey-haired man with a moustache sitting alone. He stopped without warning and brought Hong to an unceremonious halt.

"Mister Bierce?" Ming leaned toward him. "You are Ambrose Bierce, are you not?"

"Some days I wish I were not," the man grumbled.

"May I introduce us? We are the Smith Brothers."

"You're joking," said Bierce with an ironic lift of an eyebrow, looking at them from the tops of his eyes.

"I am Ming, and this is Hong. I stopped to tell you how much we enjoy your columns and especially the definitions in your Devil's Dictionary."

"Thank you," said Bierce, turning back to his lunch.

"I wondered if you ever defined 'twins.'"

Bierce opened his mouth, closed it again and thought for a few seconds. "A biological redundancy; a natal stutter, a lifetime *doppelganger*, but in your case the definition seems to be lacking."

Ming and Hong laughed and nodded to Bierce. Hong said, "Delightful. As you may guess, sir, our father had little difficulty telling us apart." At this, Bierce smiled in spite of himself. "Enjoy your lunch, sir." And as they reached their booth, Hong said to Alvin, "Please put his meal on our bill."

"Very good, sir. May I suggest the brisket *au jus.*"

"Sounds tasty," said Ming.

"For us both," said Hong. "And please bring us a bottle of good Bordeaux."

Alvin bowed and disappeared with their order.

The wine was excellent, and just before their meals arrived, Taylor crossed the dining room and came to their booth. "There's a guy hanging around outside dressed like the one by the gate."

"One of Meyung Loo's people, no doubt," said Hong. "Keep an eye on him, Taylor, but take no action unless he tries to come in."

"Right." At that moment, the waiter brought a platter of beef with sautéd onions, peas and carrots for two. Taylor's eyes drifted toward the food. "Signal me when you're coming out." The big man weaved through the tables and out the door.

"Jack," said Ming to the waiter, "Would you please have a plate taken to our coachman?"

"Very good, sir," Jack said. "The same order?"

"Yes, but instead of the Bordeaux, I think Taylor would prefer a bottle of beer."

Jack nodded and went to his task.

"Ye shall not muzzle the ox in the threshing field," said Hong.

"One of Uncle Robert's favorite Proverbs," Ming replied. "I'm sure Taylor would appreciate the sentiment, but I don't think he'd enjoy being likened to an ox."

"If the Quang-Chi monks are following us about, that means that Meyung Loo will know that we went to City Hall. If his people are aware enough, they will realize that we were meeting with Petterel. And if they are particularly observant, they will know that the ambassador was in the building, another meeting with the enemy."

"That may be how it will be construed, but Meyung must simply understand that is a part of doing business."

"Yes, but this is the West and he has an Eastern mind."

"I have an idea," said Ming, "let's set the matter aside while we enjoy this excellent beef."

"I'll second that motion. Would you pass me the pepper?"

After their meal, the brothers asked Jack to tell Taylor they were ready to leave when he went out to fetch Taylor's plate.

There was no sign of the Quang-Chi spy when Ming and Hong climbed into the carriage, and no sign of him on the trip back to the mansion. As Taylor pulled up to the gate, a dark-clad figure stepped from the trees to the side. Taylor's guns were out in a second, one aimed at Meyung Loo and the other in the opposite direction.

"It's all right, Taylor," said Hong.

Meyung Loo ignored Taylor and strode up to the gate with every ounce of dignity in his frame. He turned and glared at the brothers and pulled the bell cord.

Taylor unlocked the gate and pushed it open. As he climbed into the driver's seat, Ming said to Meyung, "Would you care to ride with us?"

Meyung snorted, "I walk."

As they rolled up the driveway, Hong said, "I hate to think it, but Meyung's man probably had the drop on Taylor when he pulled his pistols."

"And Orville had the priest in his sights at the same time."

"Wheels within wheels."

Meyung was still halfway down the driveway when Taylor pulled the carriage under the *porte-cochère*. Ming and Hong decided to wait for him before going inside. The brothers climbed out, and as they did, Raphael opened the front doors for them. To the side, Tom Hunt, a double-barreled ten-gauge shotgun under his arm, stepped around the corner of the house. He gave a short wave to Taylor and disappeared the way he had come.

"Meyung looks displeased." Said Hong.

"I'm not surprised."

XVII

Sing Chung crept down the alley behind the building that housed his office and his upstairs apartment. He had been away for two days, hiding in abandoned buildings and even sleeping under the pew of a Catholic church at the fringes of Chinatown. He was almost out of money, and almost out of hope. The Smith Brothers. Curse those freaks, he thought. When this was over and things settled down, he would deal with them.

He could go to the police for protection, but as soon as he did, Petterel would report to his Tong allies, and Sing would be found dangling from a bed sheet in his cell, or "escaped" into the arms of his pursuers. No, the only course left was to run, and to run he must first have money. Five thousand dollars lay in the safe in his office. With that money, he could escape. That amount would keep him well for years in Mexico until he found his footing again.

He looked up and down the alley and saw only a scrawny yellow dog pawing through a mound of garbage and a toothless old woman washing clothes in a tub of soapy water in a small courtyard a few doors away. From his vest pocket, Sing took a ring of keys and searched for the key to the alley door, wiping sweat from his eyes with his sleeve. His hand shook as he fumbled the key into the lock and opened the door.

Sing was greeted by dead quiet except for the ticking of the Regulator clock on the wall in the next room. He crossed the room to the small safe behind his desk, turning the keys on the ring. The door swung open and inside the safe lay the packet of bills, just as he'd left it. He breathed a sigh of relief and reached for the money."

"You have been difficult to find," a voice from behind him. Sing whirled to see a thin man in a long coat standing between him and the doorway. "Your task is incomplete, Sing Chung, and that we cannot have."

Sing Chung stared at the face of Ching Hoy, the boss of the Chinatown Tong. The alley door opened and two men came in along with the washerwoman. Ching spoke to her softly in Mandarin, smiled, put a coin in her palm and patted her hand. The old woman bowed and left. He turned back to Sing and his smile faded. "Tell me why you have not turned over the Eye."

"I—I don't have it. It was stolen from the dock—the crate."

"Ah, yes, the crate." Ching picked up a marble sphere the size of his fist with the continents carved into its surface from a three-pronged cradle on Sing's desk. He turned it over in his hands, studying it and rubbed it against the front of his vest as if he were polishing an apple.

Sing felt a trickle of cold sweat roll between his shoulder blades. "I have people looking for it…"

"The Smith Brothers?" Ching said the name like a curse. "You went to outsiders instead of coming to me, and you have cost us valuable time. And now others search for the crate. The Emperor's own men have come, and those damned priests, and the Sons of Thunder, and everyone else in Chinatown. You assured us that your methods were secure, and now, even if we find the Eye, our fee is forfeit, if not our lives. What am I to do with you, Sing Chung?"

"Then my fee is forfeit as well," said Sing quickly, throwing the money from the safe onto the desk. "It's all there, and more. Take it, please."

Ching looked at the money, idly rolling the marble globe in his fingers. He closed his eyes, and when he opened them again, Sing saw the cold reptilian gaze that earned Ching the nickname the Serpent. "That is not nearly enough to atone for your sins, Sing Chung. Perhaps there is not enough in the whole world."

He clicked his tongue and the two men behind him came forward. They grabbed Sing by the arms and slammed him onto the desk, scattering pens and blotters. The ivory inkwell tipped and ink poured over the edge of the desk like a black waterfall.

Sing's moan of terror was punctuated by his ragged breath. He made no plea. He knew it would be futile to beg for his life.

"Open his jaws." One of Ching's henchmen pulled from the top and the other from the bottom, pulling his mouth so wide that Sing's skin tore at the corners. His body thrashed and his heels pummeled the desk, but his head was unmoving.

"Greedy men want to swallow the world," said Chung, holding the marble globe contemplatively, like Hamlet with Yorick's skull. "In every case, they find their eyes too large, if not for their stomachs, certainly their throats. And your eyes have grown so very large, Sing Chung."

Ching brought the marble ball down, smashing teeth and splitting lips, forcing it into Sing Chung's mouth. He struck it with the heel of his hand, driving it down Sing's throat until it lodged there, an immovable object. Sing thrashed and convulsed briefly then lay still.

The henchmen released their grip. One of them pulled a cleaver from his coat pocket. He held Sing's lifeless wrist against the desk and with one chop, severed his right hand.

Ching picked up the money, which had fallen from the desk to the floor and nodded to his men. They slipped quietly through the door into the alley. Ching took the hand from his man, studied it for a moment, and threw it to the dog, which snatched it greedily in its jaws and ran down the alley.

XVIII

*M*ing and Hong waited on the porch for Meyung, and Taylor, instead of taking the carriage around to the carriage house, stood holding the bridle of the rightward horse and his other hand on a pistol.

"Please come in," said Ming. The brothers hung back graciously to allow Meyung to enter first. "Raphael, we will be going to our office, please bring tea." Raphael bowed and closed the doors. "Please come this way." They led Meyung to the elevator cage and he hesitated before joining them inside. He eyed the device suspiciously, but stepped into it. As they ascended, his head twitched this way and that looking in every direction as if he expected a trap to be sprung. When it stopped on the second floor, and they stepped out, he was visibly relieved.

The brothers took their seat behind the desk and Meyung sat in the wing chair as he had before, his posture almost regal.

No one spoke for a moment then Hong opened the humidor and selected a cigar. He snipped it at its center and gave half to Ming. "I would offer you one, Meyung Loo, but I suspect that you do not indulge in tobacco, or any other fleshly vice." Meyung stared at them, the corners of his mouth turning downward ever so slightly. "You disapprove of us, I think."

"You lack discipline," said Meyung in Mandarin. "I hire you to find the Eye of Quang-Chi and you insult me by meeting with my enemies and spending your day debauching yourselves with more food than a village would eat. You should be searching for the Eye at every waking moment, not wasting time as it slips further away."

"Please excuse us for not embracing the same asceticism and religious fervor as yourself," said Ming. "My brother and I are neither of your order nor of your faith. You are a holy man thrust by circumstance into an unholy business. As for how we spend our time, I would ask you, when you perform a task, does your hand act of its own accord?" Meyung stared, silent. "And does your other hand act in concert unbidden? I think not. Your mind directs your hands."

Hong broke in. "My brother and I have many hands, many eyes and many feet that do our will. You do not see them because you watch us. So too do our enemies. This is our power and our advantage. Many other parties also seek the Eye. The competition is fierce and has already erupted into violence. May I ask, was it one of your brotherhood who killed the assassin at the opera?"

"Yes," said Meyung.

"Before you engaged us?"

"We were told that you were the likeliest to find the eye in this devilish city, and we feared that if others knew our plan to enlist you, that you would come to harm before you could even begin, a way for our enemies to prevent our success. It appears that our fears were well founded."

"That places us greatly in your debt, although there were enough already who wished us dead before the Eye was ever stolen. That aside, I assure you that we are sparing neither effort nor expense in our search. I would also tell you that the police at the highest level have warned us away from helping you, at the behest of the Chinese embassy, specifically Ambassador Sen Ti."

Meyung straightened in his chair and took in a sharp breath. "The dog. He is the Emperor's personal devil. I curse him and every generation of his ancestors."

"If he has come to America to deal with this matter," said Ming, "then it must be of graver importance than even we imagined. We made it clear that we would not be deterred by threats, but what began as a simple dockside theft threatens to become an international incident."

At that moment, Raphael appeared with a tea cart. "May we offer you tea?"

XIX

*D*arby hadn't worked for the *Chronicle* for four years, but he still had keys that let him into the ground floor of its ten-story building at Kearny and Market Streets, a building that housed the newsrooms, the business offices, and the press operation all under one roof. He let himself in through the alley entrance just feet from the clattering steam powered Chandler-Price rotary presses that every day pumped out tens of thousands of copies of the largest-circulation newspaper on the West Coast.

The pressmen, busy at their tasks, paid no notice to Darby as he slipped through the racket and frenetic activity and found the door at the far end of the room that led into the bowels of the building. The door closed behind him, and the noise became as dim as the light in the corridor ahead. Ahead, an open doorway cast a dim rectangle across the floor: the morgue.

Younger, less experienced reporters shunned the morgue when they chased a story, preferring to write from their observations of the immediate event rather than gathering a context for a story. Darby quickly learned that no event stood alone, that a frame surrounded every picture, and that a good story balanced the past with the present. Unless a building was on fire or someone was bleeding out of an artery, Darby preferred to preface his news gathering with what he jokingly called an "olds gathering" in the indexed archives of the newspaper.

He rounded the doorway and found a musty room with desks and tables piled with sorted clippings. File cabinets stood in a maze of rows that filled the room, and in a far corner, a squat man with an eyeshade sat, sleeves rolled up holding a pair of scissors as long as his forearm.

"Hello, Wilbur," said Darby.

"What do you want, Darby?" said the little man without turning around.

"What do I always want, Wilbur? Information. You didn't even look. How did you know it was me?"

"That cheap Jockey Club cologne of yours came in three steps ahead of you." Wilbur turned on a rotating stool. He looked Darby up and down. He struck a match on the sole of his shoe and lit the stub of a cigar in the corner of his mouth. He blew out a puff of blue smoke. "That plaid suit makes you look like a race track tout."

"Always a pleasure." Darby crossed the room and laid a five-dollar gold piece on the worktable. Wilbur raised his eyebrows. "Try the Public Library."

"...it must be of greater importance."

"Can't smoke in the Library." Darby pulled a pint of gin out of his coat and set it beside the coin. "Sing Chung, Chinatown, and City Hall."

Wilbur stood and placed his hands at the small of his back, stretching. He pulled the stopper from the gin bottle and tipped it back, taking a swig. "Have a seat. This will take a few minutes."

Wilbur disappeared into the maze and Darby tipped the chair back against the wall. He took one of the brothers' Cuban cigars out of his pocket and cut the tip with his pocket knife. No matter who you are or what you do, thought Darby, sooner or later, you end up in the newspaper, even if it's an obituary. And the bigger you are, the thicker the file.

For all Darby knew, Wilbur lived down here; he'd never seen him out of this room. He was like a truffle pig when it came to rooting out information. The triangle: Sing Chung, the Tong, City Hall. Wilbur would supply the lines, and Darby would find their intersections. The common ground inside was where the bodies were usually buried.

Darby's cigar was half gone when Wilbur shuffled out of the maze with an armload of files. Darby held out his hands for them but Wilbur held them back. "Not so fast, buster. The price went up." He sniffed the air. "That's a damned fine cigar you're smokin'. Give me one."

"I'm glad you work so cheap," said Darby, frowning when he realized he was giving up his last Cuban.

"I'm cheap enough," said Wilbur, "but I always get what I want." He punctuated the sentence by tipping back the pint. He jerked his thumb to a table in an ill-lit corner of the morgue. "Take 'em over there. I got work to do. And put everything back the way you found it."

Darby opened the first folder. It was stuffed with clippings about the City and the "Chinese problem." The articles were in reverse chronological order from the most recent to the least, dating back for more than a decade. Darby pored over article after article about City ordinances and restrictions, vitriolic editorials about containing the expansion of Chinatown into other neighborhoods of the city, and scare pieces about yellow crime. Then he found it, an interview with Petterel about a "new era" of relations with Chinatown.

"We have too long taken an attitude toward our Chinese residents bordering on bigotry," Petterel said, "and that must cease. I want it understood that while we will continue to enforce the law to the fullest, it will be without prejudice toward any race among our residents." Darby checked the date of the article. Not an election year, so he could blow that kind of smoke without jeopardizing Collins' re-election.

Petterel went on, "I am in direct contact with a citizen's committee representing the people of Chinatown and will work with them in an attempt to improve relations between them and our police department." The second of five names was Sing Chung. Corner number one, thought Darby, licking the tip of his pencil and jotting the information into his notebook. No smoking gun, but a link nonetheless. Corner number two was Sing and the Tong, and Chang Tzu had already confirmed that connection. Where was corner number three? Any definitive link between Petterel and the Tong would be a hard proof, but if it existed, Darby was convinced it would lie in the heap of newsprint in front of him.

XX

In that "certain slant of light" Emily Dickinson celebrated in her poetry, Ming and Hong sat side by side at a concert grand piano in their music room, one of two positioned yin and yang in the great room. Their four hands flew delicately over the keys chasing the notes of Bach's "Sonata in A Major", trapping them and pressing them into the black and white keys.

As each played the delicate counterpoints, Ming in the bass range and Hong in the treble, the music swelled and filled the room, resonated with the sounding boards of violins, cellos, and violas, and made an island of peace in a brutish world. As the last chord died, Ming said. "Shall we switch?"

"Yes. Do you want to play the A major again?"

"No, let's do the 'Sonata in C'." With a nod to each other, the brothers rose and sidled away from the piano bench. They walked around one piano to the other and sat again. The second piano separated at middle C and placed the treble range to the left and the bass to the right so that an accident of birth didn't restrict either of them to half the piano.

Near the end of the piece, Raphael entered but waited respectfully until the final chord of the sonata before he spoke. "Excuse me, sirs. Orville and Tom wish to know whether you want them to stay on another night."

"I think that would be advisable," said Ming. "Do you agree?"

"Yes," said Hong. "I fear that things may become more dangerous before this affair is over."

"Very good, sirs," said Raphael, who bowed and slipped away.

"I hate to think of our home as an armed camp."

"But," said Ming, "it is the life we have chosen. *'Jeux d'enfants'*?"

"Bizet always lightens the heart."

And in moments, the brothers drifted away on a sea of bright notes, if only for a short time.

XXI

*T*he Chinaman in the chair whimpered and shook like a man with the ague. Chang Tzu pulled up a stool in front of him and put his face in front of the terrified prisoner. At the sight of Chang Tzu, he began to weep openly, for he believed that his life had already ended.

"Be a man, and you yet may live." He continued to cry and Chang struck him an openhanded blow to the side of the head that toppled him from the chair to the floor. "Stop weeping," he growled as he dragged the man to his feet and threw him back into the chair. "Do not cry, speak."

The man's breath came in ragged gasps, his eyes wide with terror.

"A crate was stolen from the docks, from the cargo of the Parma Queen, a crate with statues in it. Did you steal it?"

"No, no." The man's head shook convulsively.

"Then who?"

"I do not know. I swear on my ancestors."

"You dock rats all know each other's business. Tell me what you do know."

"I heard two men talking. One said he stole a crate with things he could not sell. I thought he was drunk. He said a horse…"

Chang grabbed the Chinaman's queue and yanked his head back. "What kind of horse?"

"I did not hear all he said, just a horse. Please! I swear!"

Chang put his knife under the prisoner's ear. "A name. What is the name of this man with a horse? Your life depends on it."

"I don't know," the man wailed. "Ling Hung! He was talking to Ling Hung, I think."

Chang looked up to his men. "A petty thief and pickpocket," said one.

Chang moved his knife to the corner of the captive's eye. "You lie, and you will not die, only wish it were so."

"No lie—no lie. I…"

"I know," said, Chang, "You swear on your damned ancestors." He stood up. "If I learn that you have warned either of these men, there is no place you can hide that I will not find you." Then to his men, "Take this blubbering woman out of here."

Two of Chang's men seized the informant by his arms and carried him, feet dragging, out the door.

"Do you think he speaks the truth?" said Lao, Chang's second-in-command.

"I know men. He would have confessed to raping my mother if it were so. He was too frightened to lie."

"So now we have a name. Ling Hung the thief."

"And soon, we shall have another." Chang sheathed his knife. "The hunt continues."

XXII

*H*alfway through one of the files, Darby found an angry letter to the *Chronicle's* editor about a "gross miscarriage of justice" in the dismissal of charges against three Chinatown men arrested for importing Chinese women for prostitution. It seems that six women got off the ship and were immediately taken to Ah Toy's and impressed into service. Six men testified at the arraignment that they were indeed the husbands of the women in question and they were delayed in reaching the dock to meet them when they embarked from the ship.

Sing Chung was one of the men released by the then chief prosecutor, Robert Petterel. The link is a long one and a strong one, thought Darby. If this was a Tong operation...

"Quitting time, Darby." Wilbur peered over his shoulder. "Find everything you need?"

"Not quite all. How's chances you let this sit 'til morning?"

"A lot better with another pint and cigar."

"Deal." Darby stood and put on his coat and hat. Past the corridor, the presses continued their clank and rattle. Some days Darby missed the news game, but most days he liked his job with the Smith Brothers much better.

In the alley, Darby turned toward Geary Street with the idea of beef and a beer at Kendrick's. Near the end of the alley, two men stepped in front of him from a dark alcove. He reached for the Derringer in his boot, and a heavy blow to the back of his head from behind put him on his knees. Rough hands rolled him over and rifled his pockets. As he lay dazed, he heard a voice rasp, "Only twenty dollars." He heard the slap of his wallet hitting the cobblestones by his head, and retreating feet, and gave up and closed his eyes.

Darby fought his way back from unconsciousness. A sleeping man could die on the street with few questions asked. His head throbbing, he crawled to a dustbin and pulled himself into a sitting position. Darby patted his coat, taking inventory. His Derringer still rested in his boot. He still had his watch. His empty wallet lay on the pavement. A wave of dread washed over him. Two things missing: his notebook and his keys. Darby flipped the case of his watch open and struck a match to see the face. Seven forty-five; he'd been out almost an hour.

He had to get to the mansion. Darby ran into Geary Street his head swiveling from side to side looking for an unoccupied cab. A couple was about to climb into a carriage at the curb in front of the music hall when Darby sprinted across the street dodging hacks and horses and vaulted into the cab from its other side. The man, a burly fellow in a suit, a laborer on holiday, shouted. "Hey! What the hell you think you're doin'?"

Darby pointed the Derringer in his face and said, "Find another ride." The man in the suit jumped back as if he'd been scalded and the cabbie's hand slid under his seat for his billy club. His hand stopped when Darby put the pistol under his ear and said, "Angle Street. Make it fast, and there's an extra fiver in it for you."

The cabbie snapped his whip and the carriage jumped from the curb, throwing Darby back into the seat as the couple stood shouting to a policeman and pointing to the retreating cab. The copper raised his whistle but realized the bounder was long gone.

XXIII

Ming and Hong stood before the chalkboard that Raphael had wheeled in an hour before. It was the old two-sided slate that Uncle Robert had used when they were boys to teach them mathematics and languages. The board was filled with names, locations, dates, and other data. Ming wrote with his left hand and Hong wrote with his right, although both were ambidextrous. They stepped back and for a long time and studied the two blocks of text, white on black.

"Ready?" said Ming.

"Yes," said Hong.

They flipped the slate to its blank side and with broad, sweeping strokes Ming drew three intersecting circles that nearly filled the board.

"Do you remember how excited Uncle Robert was when he first read of Venn diagrams?"

Hong laughed. "Yes. He couldn't wait to show the process to us. His only regret was that he didn't think of it himself." Hong smiled at the memory of the white haired old man scurrying into their office in his smoking jacket, his spectacles down his nose as if trying to escape.

"I've learned of the most useful tool I've seen in ages," he said, eyes glistening with excitement. "A way to visualize inclusion and exclusion; it is the concept of John Venn." He took the sheet of paper that Hong had been writing on, and drew three intersecting circles and labeled them A, B, and C. This section of the circle contains all those properties exclusive to set A, the overlap contains those properties shared between A and B, and A and C, subsets, if you will. The center, the Reuleaux triangle, contains all shared properties of sets A, B, and C.

"Its value lies in visualization," Uncle Robert said. "A tool for deduction."

"How many sets can such a diagram include?" said Ming.

"Three at most," said Uncle Robert, "but I will experiment with other geometric figures to see whether it may be expanded to greater numbers."

"And mathematicians have been wrestling with the unholy trinity ever since." said Hong. "In the decade since Venn published his paper, no one has solved the conundrum to anyone's satisfaction. I must confess, however, that it is a useful method to visualize a problem."

"Three will suffice for today. Let us begin."

In the A circle, Ming wrote "Sing Chung"; in the B circle, "Meyung Loo"; and in the C circle, "The Emperor". "I think that will do for the moment," he said. "So, where do A and B overlap?"

"Both have approached us to find something." Hong made a notation in the AB region. "Sing has other affiliations; Meyung Loo has none that we know." He wrote, "Tong?" in A.

"Do we also include Tong ties to the Emperor?" said Ming.

"Meyung Loo says yes, but we have no direct evidence. I'd say we should hold that assumption for the moment."

In A, Hong wrote "money"; in B, he wrote "religion"; in C, he wrote "power". "And in the intersection of those conflicting motives," he said, "we find the Eye of Quang-Chi." He wrote the word "Eye" in the center section of the diagram.

"Ming wrote "Police" in C and after a moment's hesitation, "Petterel".

"And where do our would be assassins lurk in this diagram?"

Ming tapped the chalk against his teeth. "The first attempt occurred before we interacted with A or B." He wrote "assassin?" under Petterel's name.

"That begs the question," said Hong. "Was Petterel behind one attempt, both, or neither?"

"I would not accuse him out of hand, but neither would I discount the possibility. That may become clearer as the skein unwinds."

The gate bell rang. The brothers went to the window and saw three men in the lamplight, two in uniform. "Police," said Ming.

"Not Hawkins this time, said Hong. None of them is big enough."

"Shall we go downstairs?"

"No, let them come to us. Help me cover the chalkboard." The brothers pulled an embroidered silk throw from a nearby divan and draped it over their work. Raphael soon appeared in the doorway. "Sirs, a Detective Harmon and two patrolmen wish to speak to you."

"Bring Detective Harmon up, please," said Hong, "and ask the others to wait in the foyer."

"Very good, sirs." Raphael left, and Hong pulled a pair of files from the desk drawer, spreading their contents over the desk. "Look busy."

Raphael brought all three men upstairs but stood in the doorway barring their entrance. "Sirs, the detective insisted that his men accompany him."

"It's all right, Raphael," said Ming. "Let them come in."

The policemen entered, and the brothers stood. The officers' eyes darted around the room, but Harmon's gaze was fixed on his hosts. Like many of San Francisco's finest, he harbored a resentment for the "rank amateurs" who solved crimes ahead of the police.

"Detective Harmon," said Hong. "How may we help you?"

Harmon was short and heavy-set, not quite fat but on his way. His thatch of dirty blond hair trailed from his bowler hat into a pair of reddish brown mutton chop sideburns that gave him an unfinished look, like partially ripened fruit. "A man was murdered today." He paused as if what he had said were profound. "In Chinatown. Seems you knew him."

"And who is this man?" said Ming.

"He had your business card in his wallet," Harmon went on, not allowing his prepared script to be rushed. "I need to know whether he was a client of yours."

"And his name?"

"Sing Chung." Harmon watched the brothers' faces, waiting for reaction, but seeing none. "Well, was he a client of yours?"

"No," said Ming. "He was not."

"Then why was he carrying your card with him?"

"Detective, we are in business. Our cards circulate from hand to hand. I cannot account for..." The uniformed officers had begun strolling around the room, and one of them picked up a jade statue from the mantel. "Do you have a search warrant?" Hong snapped at the man.

"Uh, no."

"Then touch nothing."

The officer looked to Harmon who gave a curt nod. "This man Sing Chung, did you ever meet him?"

"Yes," said Ming.

"Well why didn't you say so?" said Harmon, his face flushing.

"Because you didn't ask the question. Now, if I may ask one, what were the circumstances of Sing Chung's death?"

Ignoring the question, Harmon said, "How did you know him?"

"He came here wishing to employ us. We declined."

"Why?"

"Such matters are confidential, Detective."

"Don't pull that line with me, Smith; you refused him. He wasn't your client, so there is no confidentiality. Now tell me what he wanted."

"The Detective is correct," said Hong. "Yet, the Constitution provides us the sanctity of our home and our private business."

"Perhaps a *quid pro quo*." Ming turned to Harmon. "If we tell you what you wish to know, will you tell us the details of the murder?"

"Oh what the hell. It'll all be in the papers tomorrow. Goddamned muckrakers got there ahead of us."

Ming took cigarettes for himself and Hong from the case on the desk. He offered one to Harmon, who took two, lighting one and slipping one in his pocket for later. "You first."

"It is very simple, really," said Hong. "Sing came to us because some property of his was stolen. We made enquiries, and determined that we could do nothing to help him; thus we did not take his case."

"What was stolen?"

"A crate containing art objects, apparently stolen from the dock when it was unloaded."

"Sing said he reported it to the police. Surely there is a report on file."

"Not that I know of, but I'll look into it."

"Now, please tell us about the murder," said Ming. "Perhaps we may still be of some help," Harmon looked at the end of his cigarette, as if the answer to the question were written on its glowing tip. "Sing was smothered to death. Actually, his throat was clogged with a marble ball."

"Were there other injuries?"

"Yeah, you could say that," said one of the coppers, a beefy red-faced brute with a bristling moustache. "Somebody chopped off his right hand and took it with him."

Harmon turned and glared at the man, annoyed at being upstaged by an underling.

"And what does that suggest to you?" asked Ming.

"That maybe he crossed the Tong, or the Sons of Thunder, or any of the gangs in Chinatown."

"Was anything stolen?" said Hong?

The safe was open and there was nothing in it but papers."

"Sing was well known at City Hall, was he not?"

Harmon nodded. "Yeah. He was a part of the Chinatown Citizens' Committee to assist the police. That's why the heat's on us to find out who did it."

"Rest assured that we will alert you to any information we may encounter in this matter," said Ming.

"Appreciate it," said Harmon. "It's obvious to me that you two didn't personally kill him, but just the same, make yourselves available." He motioned to his officers. "Let's go."

Hong pulled the bell rope. "Raphael will show you out."

Ming and Hong waited until the policemen were outside the gate before uncovering the blackboard. "This changes things," said Ming, studying the Venn diagram. He picked up a thick felt eraser and in three broad strokes removed circle A.

XXIV

*T*he carriage stopped in front of the mansion. Darby said to the cabbie, "Wait." Remembering Darby's pistol, the cabbie didn't argue. Darby whistled between his fingers and Orville stepped from the shadows, a rifle under his arm.

"Got a five?"

"Orville grunted and reached into his coat for his wallet. He chose a bill and handed it to Darby, through the gate and Darby passed it to the cabbie. "Forget you ever came here."

The cabbie's response was to snap his whip and drive off as quickly as possible from the men and their guns.

"Has there been any trouble?" Darby spoke through the bars.

Orville shook his head. "Nope. Been quiet." He spat his tobacco juice onto the driveway.

"That may change. I got rolled and they took my keys. You might tell Tom and Taylor to watch the back."

Orville said in a low voice. "Already covered. Don't look and give him away; Tom's on the roof above the turret."

"Open the gate, would you, Orville."

"Can't, Darby. Only Raphael and Taylor have the key. My job's to keep people out, not let them in."

Darby rolled his eyes pulled the bell rope.

At the end of the driveway, Darby could see the rectangle of light as Raphael opened the front door to come outside.

At the sound of the gate bell, Ming and Hong went to the window and saw Darby standing on the street.

"That is odd," said Ming. "Why would Darby need to ring the bell?"

"I suspect we'll find out soon."

Darby came into the office moments later, hatless, a knee torn in the trousers of his green plaid suit. His usual casual demeanor was gone, replaced by a sense of urgency.

"My keys. They took my keys."

"Darby," said Ming, "sit down." The brothers crossed to the liquor cart and poured three fingers of whiskey into a tumbler and handed it to Darby. He drank half of it in one pull.

"Now," said Hong, "tell us what happened."

"I was digging in the morgue at the *Chronicle*. When I left, three guys jumped me. It was dark and I got sapped pretty good. They took the cash out of my wallet, my ring of keys and my notebook, but they left my watch and my ring. He held up his hand to show the heavy silver ring with the letter D set into onyx."

"A clumsy attempt to mask their true intentions with the pretense of a simple mugging," said Ming. "What was in the notebook?"

"The old one was about full, so I used a new one today. It had everything

I found about Sing and Petterel. They have a past going back to the days when Petterel was Chief Prosecutor." He drank the second half of his whiskey. "What worries me is the key ring. If they can get in here…"

Hong raised a hand. "There is no immediate threat. Orville and Tom have the property under watch. What concerns me is not our keys, but yours. You should go to your flat immediately. Take Taylor with you, and see whether they have been there. If they haven't, wait."

He pulled the bell cord, gave Raphael instructions, and poured Darby another whiskey.

"You didn't see the thieves," said Hong, "but did they say anything?"

Darby rubbed the knot at the back of his head. "I did hear one of them complain that I had only twenty bucks in my wallet."

"Did you know the voice?"

"Nope. But now that I think about it, there was no accent. He talked like a local."

"Another player in the game," said Ming.

"Perhaps, or simply someone on hire by the others."

Taylor appeared in the doorway, already in his coat.

"Taylor, accompany Darby to his flat," said Ming. "Darby will give you instructions. And when you are finished, please bring him back here."

"And Taylor, please give Darby a more formidable firearm."

When they left, Hong said, "What should we do about the locks?"

"I think we should leave them unchanged. It might be interesting to see who uses Darby's keys."

The brothers returned to the chalkboard. They stared at it for a while, then Ming redrew the erased circle and in it drew a question mark.

XXV

*T*aylor led Darby to a steel door at a far corner of the basement that Darby had never seen. Taylor unlocked the door from a heavy ring of keys and it swung open. He lit the lamp and Darby saw a collection of weapons that would rival the Police station. Rifles and shotguns rested in orderly ranks along one wall. A brass hand mortar from pirate days sat on a canister of explosive shells.

Wall mounts held every type of hand weapon Darby had ever seen and many that were new to him. Brass knuckles, Samurai swords and *tantos*, Bowie knives and daggers, straight bladed poniards hung with wavy *kris*, and hooked Gurkha *kukris* made for beheading.

From the pistol wall, Taylor chose an oversized hand gun, a bigger version of Darby's Derringer with over-under barrels. Taylor opened the chamber and slid two long shells into it. He snapped it shut and handed it and a half-dozen shells to Darby.

"This fires two .410 shotgun shells same way as your Derringer. Hold it with both hands. You make sure I'm nowhere in front of you when you pull the trigger. It'll knock down three men at six feet easy. Just point and fire. Aim ain't exactly crucial."

Taylor pulled a Bowie knife from its sheath and opened Darby's coat. Before he could ask Taylor what he was doing, Taylor slashed the coat's lining and cut the bottom seam from his pocket. "Hold the gun under your coat through the pocket. You might be slow getting it out of your waistband without practice."

The carriage was waiting under the portico. Taylor climbed into the driver's seat and laid a pump shotgun across his thighs and covered it with a lap robe. "Sit in the seat facing the back," he said. I'll watch forward, you watch behind."

As the carriage rolled through the gate, Darby's grip tightened on the pistol under his coat. With his free hand, he fumbled a cigarette from his pocket and put it in his mouth. The first match he struck blew out because he couldn't cup his hand around it. It took two more tries before he got his cigarette lit.

Darby had been working for the Smith Brothers for four years, yet he never quite got used to being in the middle of peril instead of just writing about it after the fact. But, he thought, if I run into more trouble, there aren't many people I'd rather have with me than Taylor.

The trip to Darby's flat was slow going because the streets were crowded. Theaters had let out and throngs of people were spilling off the sidewalks onto the street. Taylor threaded the carriage through the traffic easily enough, though, and soon they were slipping along the side streets to Darby's door. The windows of the second floor flat were dark, and only a few people walked from lamp to lamp on Carmody Street.

The pair climbed down from the carriage, Taylor holding his shotgun down at his side, his head slowly turning one way then another, scanning the street.

Seeing that no one was looking their way, Taylor put his foot to the

"..two more tries before he got his cigarette lit."

door and it swung inward with a sharp crack. He motioned Darby inside then followed, closing the door behind him. He raised the gun to the top of the darkened staircase and said quietly. "Strike a match and hold it away from your body.

The match flared and Darby saw an empty stairwell and landing outside his flat. Taylor gestured with the shotgun, Darby blew out the match, and they slowly climbed the narrow steps. At the top, Darby's door was closed. He turned the knob. The door was unlocked. Darby held his breath as he reached around the doorjamb to the gaslight and turned the key.

"Don't shoot me, Darby." Chang Tzu slouched in an armchair, his arms folded across his chest. With the exception of Chang's chair, every item in the room was pulled down, upended or emptied onto the floor. He shrugged. "I was looking for a match."

"In the kitchen above the wash basin."

Taylor relaxed. "Chang," he said, nodding.

"Taylor," said Chang. "We all seem to have missed the party."

Darby nodded. "I was mugged and the bastards took my keys."

"Yes, the doors were both locked when I came. Of course that was little problem for me."

"Why did you relock the street door?"

"So I would hear you when you came in. It was unnecessary, however. You might have been more stealthy if you had ridden horses up the stairs."

"I'm surprised to see you outside Chinatown," Darby said, righting a divan. He shook his head at the slashed seat cushion, batting bursting out of the damask like popcorn.

"Sometimes the mountain must come to Mohammed. I would have sent for you, but there is now a thousand dollar bounty for you on the street. At that amount, if you came to me, you might not arrive."

"Dead or alive?" said Taylor.

"Oh most definitely not dead," said Chang. "You are to be taken alive."

"Who wants me that bad?"

"The arrangement is being brokered by the Tong on behalf of persons unspecified. You have angered someone greatly, or perhaps simply inconvenienced him. Chinatown is restless. Something very large is happening under the surface, even beyond my knowledge. Be watchful, Darby. Not many of my friends in Chinatown like to drink bourbon."

A noise in the stairwell made Taylor wheel around and jack a shell in the chamber of the shotgun.

Chang said something in Mandarin and was answered from below.

"My men," he said in English. "They were watching the door from across the street."

"What about the crate?" said Darby.

"The crate has become a subject of much discussion in many quarters. We have an inkling as to who may have stolen it, but as yet, it has not been found. However, the fervor with which others continue to seek it suggests that they have not found it either."

"If I can't come safely to Chinatown, how do I contact you?"

"Send a message to Tim Soo. I will get it." He rose. "Now, if you will excuse me, I have to return to Chinatown. My protection from the police does not extend to this neighborhood." Chang nodded to Darby and Taylor and disappeared down the stairs.

Darby and Taylor spent the next two hours righting furniture, replacing drawers, and returning their contents. The burglars had been thorough, going so far as to dump the canisters of tea and coffee in the tiny kitchen, and even Darby's can of tooth powder beside the pitcher and lave.

"So, what's missing?"

"My notebooks. All of them. I've been keeping notes on every case the Brothers solved. I wanted to maybe write stories like that Doyle guy in England. Well, I guess now I'll just have to rely on my memory."

XXVI

*M*ing and Hong sat before the fire on the divan in the upstairs parlor, Ming with his flute and Hong with his cello. Bach's *Watchet Auf* rang through the halls of the mansion. As the last notes faded, Hong said, "I think it is time we go back to the diagram."

"Or perhaps draw a new one."

Downstairs, they stood studying the chalkboard. Hong picked up the eraser and cleared the slate. He redrew the intersecting circles. In A, he wrote "The Emperor"; in B, "Meyung Loo", and in C, "Police."

"I concur."

Hong wrote in the intersection of A and C "Ambassador Sen Ti."

"Since he requested, no, demanded that we not pursue Meyung's case, I believe that Sen Ti belongs in the center of the diagram." Ming moved Sen Ti to the middle section.

"Very well; if Sen Ti is at the center of the matter, his position points to the Emperor as the root of the problem."

"Which would confirm Meyung's story of the Emperor's involvement with the Eye as a political tool."

Hong nodded. And the Eye of Quang-Chi — does it lie between A and B? Or does Petterel's involvement put it in the center as well?"

"Let us say yes." Ming said, moving the Eye to the center. "That puts Sen Ti and the Eye together."

"Yes," said Hong. "But he is no everyday person. Digging into his affairs will be no easy matter."

"That is where Darby can be of service."

"But Darby has become as much a target as we these past few days. He can't move as freely as he had."

"But we are not totally without resources ourselves," said Ming. "We have access to maritime information. We should be able to determine when Sen Ti has traveled between here and China in the last three months."

"True. Until now, the Eye was the hub of this wheel. Now it shares that distinction with Sen Ti."

Ming drew a curved slash between the two names, dividing the triangle. "Like Yin and Yang."

XXVII

*W*on Lao tried to look at anything else in the room, the chair, the table, the goods that were stacked against the wall, things he had stolen or bought from addicts to feed their opium habits. But his gaze inevitably returned to the terra cotta horse and the porcelain urn. He cursed the foul luck that of all the crates on the dock he had stolen the one that stood beside them.

The wiry little man had slipped out of the fog disguised as a longshoreman with a hand cart, rolling a crate filled with refuse onto the dock where the Parma Queen was being unloaded. He nodded to the watchman, whom he had paid off earlier that day and wound his way down the aisles between the crates, bales and cases from the ship's hold.

He found a crate almost exactly the same size, set his down, replaced it with the Parma Queen's crate and wheeled it past the watchman, who studiously looked at nothing in particular. Down the alley and onto his waiting wagon and no one the wiser. The right number of crates still stood on the dock. No one would notice the theft for days.

Now the opened crate stood in his shanty, and its contents stood beside it, mocking him. He could fence neither the urn, nor the statue. Word was out on the street that the Tong were looking for just such a crate, the Tong and others. Everyone in Chinatown seemed to be looking for it, and here it stood, a millstone around his neck. At one minute, he thought he might strike a deal, ransom the crate and its contents, and the next he realized that whatever interest lay in the crate had to be illegal, and the Tong abided no witnesses to their wrongdoing.

Won came to a decision. He must remove any evidence of the theft, and he must do it now. He picked up the hammer that lay on his workbench. He would pound the horse and the urn to dust, then he would pull the crate apart and burn the wood in his stove, the marked pieces first, removing any evidence of his act.

How sad, he thought, gazing at the horse and rider in the glow from his wood stove; a warrior who would never reach his battle, his destiny unfulfilled. The first blow was the hardest to strike, not because Won Lao loved fine art, but because he loved the money that it might have brought. The hammer struck the horse's head and it shattered, scattering shards across the stones of the floor. Won crouched and struck one of the shards once, twice, three times, reducing it to russet-colored dust. The second blow was easier, as were the third, the fourth, and the fifth until the horse and rider were no more.

Won Lao was sweating now. He turned to the urn, and raised his hammer.

XXVIII

"Will there be anything else, sirs?" Raphael said, taking the tray with the brandy and snifters.

"Thank you, no, Raphael." The butler nodded and left the office.

Darby took a long, thoughtful pull at his cigar. "I guess they didn't find what they wanted in the notebook they took when they mugged me."

"Or they simply wanted them all to sift at their leisure," said Ming. "You are sure nothing else was stolen."

"Not a thing. If they were just burglars, they could have taken things like my spare cuff links, the coins on my dresser, my mantel clock. All they wanted was information."

"Can you return to the newspaper office tomorrow? We can send Taylor with you."

"I lost my keys to the *Chronicle* building with all the others. I can't slip in unnoticed now, and I'm not exactly welcome there these days. I hear Michael deYoung personally ordered that I'm not allowed on the premises. His security people would likely drag me down the front steps by my ankles."

"Could you find what you need in the Public library?" said Hong. "Surely they have newspapers on file, and the *Chronicle* is the most prominent."

Darby nodded in agreement. "It would be slow going, but, yeah. I might be able to pick up where I left off."

"We have another subject for you to pursue," said Ming. "Ambassador Sen Ti."

"Yes," said Hong. "Particularly any connection between him and Petterel."

"Okay. I'll get on it tomorrow morning."

Darby left for his room, and the brothers sat at their desk. Ming looked across to the chalkboard. "We left something out of the diagram in Sen Ti's section."

"What is that, brother?"

"Diplomatic immunity."

"That could be a problem."

"For the police, not for us."

"And certainly not for Chang."

"My thoughts exactly."

They climbed the stairs to the master bedroom, forgoing the elevator. In contrast to the opulence of the rest of the house, the room was Spartan, dominated by a large canopied bed. Raphael had turned the covers down, and dimmed the light. The brothers undressed and sat nude at the foot of the bed. Hong held his pistol in his right hand.

"What are you going to do with that?" said Ming. "That's a problem with sleeping naked. You don't have a convenient pocket to put it in."

"I'll keep it under my pillow."

"I hope you don't have a nightmare and shoot off my ear in your sleep."

They leaned back onto the bed and with their feet, pushed themselves to the headboard. They pulled the covers to their chins.

"Tomorrow is another day," said Ming.

"Yes, and it will be at least as interesting as this one."

"Something continues to nag at me," said Ming. If Sing Chung and the Tong knew when the crate would arrive, how did they allow it to be stolen?"

"Perhaps we will learn the answer to that question tomorrow. Good night."

In moments, the brothers were asleep, each dreaming of walking alone.

XXIX

Won Lao swept the dust into a mound on the floor. Flecks of glaze sparkled in the light from his pot bellied stove. It had taken him more than an hour to pulverize the urn and the horseman. He was weary, but for the first time in days, he felt a sense of relief. By morning every trace of his crime would be gone. Now to the crate.

The nails screeched as Won pried the first board from the side and twisted it free. The crate was sturdy, and its inside was sealed with a coating of tar, which made the job even more difficult. Excelsior clung to the board and dangled like the tendrils of a jellyfish. The board was too thick to break over his knee, so he had to split it long ways with a hatchet and chop it to kindling to feed into the stove.

Another board and another. Won pried at a board and read again the name of the intended recipient painted in Mandarin and in English on the rough wood: Sing Chung. A small comfort, that; Sing Chung had plied his influence and extracted his toll on Won until he drove him out of his legitimate business and forced him into a life of crime. Won laughed bitterly. If he could not profit from the statue and the urn, at least Sing would not benefit from them either.

A sound behind him. Won turned to see three men like silent shadows in the dim firelight. He sprang to his feet screaming and threw himself at the intruders, swinging the hatchet. One of the men put up a defensive arm, and Won felt the bone snap under the wicked edge. Before he could pull the blade free, strong arms seized him and threw him to the floor.

The injured man fell to his knees, blood pumping from a severed artery. He stared at his life running away from him like a man who watches a ship he has missed sailing away from the harbor. From behind him came another man, one whom Won Tao recognized, the Tong boss Ching Hoy, and his blood froze. His hour had come.

Won did not scream. In his heart, he knew it would come to this, if not tonight, tomorrow, or next week, or next year.

Ching Hoy walked around the crate studying it from all sides. Then he saw the mound of dust. He bent down and took a handful of it, sniffed at it, and sifted it through his fingers. "Like the sand in an hourglass," he said in Mandarin. "Your time runs out quickly. How you will spend that time, in pleasure or in pain depends on you, Won Tao."

"You will kill me," said Won. "I know this. Get it over with."

"But," said Ching, drawing a small leather pouch from his pocket. "Will you depart with pleasant visions, or with screams of agony? A pinch of this..." he hefted the bag in his palm. "Will put your mind in another place. Where is the gem?"

Won Tao's head rolled from side to side in confusion. "Gem? What gem?"

Ching Hoy smiled. "As you wish," and to his men. "Bind him and search this pigsty."

Ching's men hauled Won onto the only chair in the room. They bound his ankles to the chair legs and tied his hands behind his back to the slats of the chair. "Do not gag him," said Ching. "He may change his mind."

"I don't know what you're talking about," said Won.

"Oh, but you do," said Ching, plucking a long shard of wood from the floor. He held it in the stove, and the tar caught instantly, crackling and bubbling. Ching passed it slowly back and forth before Won's eyes. Behind him, Won heard the crash of glass and the splintering of wood as the Tong thugs ransacked his inventory. "Tell me, Won, where is the gem? Purchase yourself a peaceful end."

"I know of no gem."

Ching held the burning wood to the end of Won Tao's drooping moustache. The hair caught and climbed quickly to his face. With a thumb and forefinger, Ching snuffed the flame just before it reached Won's upper lip. "I will ask again in a moment. Please consider your answer carefully."

"There is no gem. I found only the horse and the urn in the crate."

Ching tipped his head to the side as if thinking. "Crate? I mentioned no crate."

"The talk is all over Chinatown that you seek a crate."

"I think you know more than you tell me, Won Tao. Shortly, I will find out." Ching took a rag from the work table and stuffed it into Won's mouth. He looked into the prisoner's eyes and saw no terror. Time enough for that. The night is young.

Ching leaned against the table and lit a cigarette, watching his men methodically dismantle everything in the room. "*Hai!*" cried one of them. He pulled up a loose board from the floor. Instead of looking at the hole, Ching looked at Won's eyes and saw sadness, not fear, a fine distinction. Ching had learned over time to read men through their eyes, and he was seldom incorrect.

Mei Wat, the bigger of Ching's henchmen reached under the floor and drew out a small leather satchel.

"Bring it here."

Ching dumped the satchel onto the table. A wad of banknotes tumbled out, along with some gold coins and an assortment of watches, rings, and other jewelry. He rummaged through them but found no ruby.

"The time has come for you to speak," said Ching, pulling the rag from Won's mouth. "Where is the gem? Is it here? Or does someone else now have it?"

"I know nothing of any gem," Won said, his voice becoming plaintive. "I swear it."

"Perhaps it is on his person. Strip him."

Sharp knives cut Won's clothing to rags. Pockets were turned out, seams were opened, but to no avail. Around Won's neck, Ching saw a thin leather thong. On it hung a copper coin with a square hole in its center. He took the coin between his thumb and forefinger and turned it over. "The five poisons; the scorpion, the spider, the centipede, the toad and the snake. But there is a force greater than all of these, and against it there is no protection. That force is the lightning of the Tong."

Ching lit another splint in the stove and held it before Won's face. Without speaking, he set the other side of Won's moustache afire, but this time, he let it burn. The flame danced for a second or two under Won's eye, then died, filling his nostrils with the smell of charred flesh and burnt hair.

Ching's eyelids drooped and the corners of his mouth turned down in mock pity. "What an unpleasant stench." He looked around the room and saw an incense holder with a half-burned stick of incense in it. He held the incense to his nose. "Jasmine. That will do." He lit the stick in the stove and set it in the holder.

Ching walked around the room, picking up one thing and another, then setting them down again. He reached into the crate and pulled out a handful of excelsior. He studied it for a moment, turning the mass over in his hands like a tangled ball of twine. He wadded the excelsior between Won's knees and lit another splint from the stove. "Tell me, Won Lao."

"I cannot tell you what I do not know," said Won, his eyes transfixed on the flame from the splint.

"Your choice," said Ching. The flame leapt from the splint into the excelsior, which burst into a bright ball of flame. Won gritted his teeth and grunted with pain. He would not scream. He would not give his tormentors the satisfaction. Even the incense could not mask the odor.

Ching took another ball of excelsior from the crate. This he wadded in Won's groin. He did not speak, but picked up the burning splint again, holding it like a magician's wand. He waved it close to the excelsior, once, twice, three times, teasing Won. Then he lit the excelsior, and this time, Won did scream.

Ching held the small leather pouch in front of Won's pain glazed eyes. "The dust of dreams. I can take away your pain if only you will tell me what I want to know."

"I can tell you nothing," whispered Won, his breath coming in ragged gasps.

"He has held fast up to now, because he knows that we will not find the jewel in this hovel and has endured great pain to keep his secret. There is only one place left to look. He has either swallowed the gem somehow, or forced it into his bowels. Cut him open. But do not kill him—yet."

XXX

It had taken the Sons of Thunder more than a day to find Ling Hung and less than a minute to coerce the pickpocket to supply the name of the man who could not fence a horse. And now Chang and his men threaded through the dark alleys of Chinatown to Won Lao's hideout.

A light shone around the shutter of the shanty's single window. Chang signaled to his men, and one took a position on either side of the door. Min Li aimed a shotgun at the doorway as Chang lifted the latch. The door swung inward on its own weight. From inside, he heard only the crackle of wood in the stove. Chang drew his pistol and stepped across the threshold, Min Li behind him, the shotgun barrel resting on Chang's shoulder.

Chang saw the dark footprints first, then the crate, then the heap of dust; then his eye fixed on the mound of red flesh on the table. He found a pencil and paper in the scattered rubble on the floor. He wrote a note and folded the paper. "Take this to Darby at the Smith Brothers' home. Wait for a reply." Min Li nodded. Chang stepped outside the shanty to breathe cleaner air. To his guards he said, "Let no one enter, including the police." He looked overhead at the sprinkling of stars visible between the buildings that lined the alley, took a last lungful of air, and went back inside.

XXXI

Ming shook Hong. "Wake up. The gate bell."

The bell rang again insistently. The brothers rose from their bed and dressed quickly. Before they were finished, Raphael came into the room. "Sirs, a messenger from Chang Tzu, with a message for Darby. I felt I should speak with you first.

"Is Darby awake?" Ming said.

"No, sir."

"Then wake him and tell him of our visitor, then go to the gate and ask him to wait. Tell him Darby will join him shortly."

"Very good, sir." Raphael disappeared down the corridor.

"Aren't we taking a chance to have Darby go to the gate?" Hong said.

"You mean if it isn't really Chang's man? If he makes a wrong move, Orville or Tom will put holes in him."

"If Meyung's friend in the bushes doesn't get him first."

Downstairs, Darby was waiting in the foyer in his shirtsleeves, his suspenders hanging from his waist. He looked as if he had just tumbled out of bed while Ming and Hong looked as if they were just leaving for the office. Behind Darby, the hall clock struck three.

"Must be important, huh?" he said.

"Important enough," said Hong. "Go see what he has to say."

Darby nodded and opened the door. "Here goes nothin'." He slipped into his coat and clutched the .410 pistol through the torn pocket.

Ming and Hong watched his silhouette as he walked down the driveway. At the gate, a man stepped from the shadows. They spoke for a moment, and the messenger handed Darby something then stepped back into the shadows away from the gate lamp.

Darby returned with a sheet of paper in his hand. "It was Chang's man, Min Li." He brought this note.

Well," said Ming, "What does it say?"

"Chang has found the crate."

"Good news." said Hong.

"But not the gem."

"How disappointing."

"It seems someone got there first, but they may not have it either."

"Why so?"

"Their search was extremely thorough." Darby wiped sweat from his brow. "Including the thief's entrails."

"But was it thorough enough?" Hong said. "Tell your friend we would see for ourselves," then to Raphael, "Tell Taylor to bring the carriage around."

"I don't know if Min Li will agree to that."

"Be persuasive."

Darby went back to the gate as Taylor brought the carriage to the portico. There was some argument and forceful gesturing, but finally Darby waved his arm, and Ming and Hong climbed into the carriage. They stopped at the gate and Taylor jumped down to unlock it as Darby climbed in. The carriage rolled out into the street and Ming said to Min Li in Mandarin, "Join us, my friend. The journey will be shorter."

After a brief hesitation, Min Li climbed into the carriage and sat beside Darby.

"Tell us, please," said Hong, "which way do we go?"

Min Li said simply, "Chinatown."

The fog was rolling in from the bay and the city was slowly disappearing into a dim haze punctuated by the glow of the gas lights along the street. The closer they came to Chinatown, the dimmer the city became.

No one spoke as they moved through the dark streets. They saw no one but felt eyes upon them at every turn. It was as if Chinatown held its breath while dangerous creatures circled each other in the black and crawling night.

"Tell us when we are close," said Ming to Min Li. "We will stop the carriage and walk."

Min Li nodded acknowledgement and turned to give direction to Taylor. After a few more twists and turns through alleys and byways, he said, "Here."

Taylor reined the horses. Min Li hopped out of the carriage, a pistol suddenly in his hand. His head swiveled one way and the other. "Quickly. Follow me."

The twins and Darby stepped out of the carriage onto the rough cobbles of the street. "Wait here," Hong said to Taylor.

"Will you be all right alone?"

"We have Darby," said Ming, "and these." From beneath their cloak, both brothers drew short barreled pump shotguns. To emphasize the point, Ming racked a shell into the chamber.

A short distance away from Won Lao's shanty, Min Li brought the party to a halt. "I must go alone first. If my friends see a group of men when they expect one, they may shoot without pause." He disappeared into the shadows.

"Did it ever occur to you that we may be walking into a trap?" said Darby?"

Ming replied. "There are days when one must have faith. Chang has always dealt honorably with us—when we pay him."

"The Eye is a temptation," said Hong, "in more ways than one. It could be cut and sold for quite a sum, or it could be ransomed to the highest bidder, or Chang could use it as leverage against the Tong. I suspect that if Chang found it and he wanted the stone for himself, he would have left the Tong's work to be found, we would assume that they have the Eye, and we would pursue a false trail."

"Wheels within wheels," said Ming.

Two figures materialized in the fog. Min Li and Chang.

"Why have you come?" Chang said his voice as emotionless as if he were asking a passing stranger for the time.

"Each eye sees differently, my friend," said Hong. Perhaps we might see what others have not. After all, we all seek the same end, do we not?"

Chang pondered this then said. "Very well, but your safety is your own responsibility."

"Agreed."

"Then follow me." Chang led them through the maze of alleys while Min Li followed with his pistol in hand, eyes darting to every shadow, alert for any threat. They came to the ramshackle building to find Chang's men guarding the door.

The brothers had to move sideways through the narrow portal. Once inside, they stopped. Ming pointed to the floor. "These tracks, were they here when you arrived?"

"Yes, but I cannot guarantee that I and my people did not add to them."

"At least three men." said Ming.

Darby stepped around them and felt his gorge rising at the sight of Won Lao's corpse on the table like a subject in a Vesalius woodcut. "Jesus. I've seen autopsies, but at least they put everything back where they found it."

"Look there," said Hong. "More blood." The brothers crouched beside it and Hong drew a finger through the stain. "Still sticky. There seems to be too much of it to have come from him," Hong gestured at the table.

"Won Lao," said Chang. "He was a dock rat, a thief and a small-time broker who paid addicts for what they could steal."

"Won Lao," said Hong, "has bled copiously on the table and onto the floor. Someone else has bled here, and likely died, based on the amount of blood. Perhaps Won Lao did not go to his grave alone."

"Possibly one of the Tong," said Ming. "The blood is smeared, but not much. The man was lifted and carried out. If he were a confederate of Won's they would have left him."

Ming and Hong walked around the table, careful to not disturb the dark footprints on the floorboards.

"'From his nave to his chaps,'" said Ming.

"What?" said Darby.

"Shakespeare," said Ming. "That Scottish play. He has been, as you said Darby, very thoroughly examined. Every inch of his alimentary canal has been opened. They thought he swallowed the Eye."

"Is that possible? Isn't it too large?" Darby said, looking pointedly away from the mass of entrails.

"Won Lao was a thief," said Chang. "He surely knew every trick of his trade. I have known men who have trained themselves to swallow things others would find impossible."

"Like a carnival performer," said Ming. "Yes, he could have swallowed the gem. And the Tong may have found it, but I do not believe they have."

"I agree," said Hong. "One always finds what he seeks in the last place he looks. The stone was not in his stomach, the first place to look, nor in his bowels." He pointed to the grey loops of intestine that lay to the side of the gutted body. "Every inch of his intestine has been slit. If they had found the gem, they would have stopped immediately."

Hong's eyes traveled from one end of the corpse to the other. "He was tortured. Burned rather badly. And he did not tell them what they wanted to know. If he confessed to swallowing the gem, they would have taken him with them and simply waited for nature to take its course rather than cut him open. I wonder...help me turn him over."

They turned the corpse onto what was left of its stomach. Won Lao's skin stuck to the table and made a noise like ripping wet cloth as it pulled away. "What are we looking for?" Darby said.

"Stitches."

"Yes, he could have swallowed the gem."

The brothers bent over the corpse. "The Parma Queen docked three days ago. If he cut himself to hide the stone under his skin, the incision would still be healing, however small."

"Nothing," said Ming. "I think we can safely say that he did not have the stone in his body."

"Then let us examine the room."

"What could you find that the Tong did not?" said Chang.

"I don't know yet, but as I said, other eyes."

Darby held up the empty satchel. "Looks like they cleaned this out." He put his hand inside. "Wait." He pulled out a gold ring with a small emerald setting. "This was caught in the lining."

"So they took his loot for their trouble," said Ming. "Turn out the lining."

"Nothing else."

"I wouldn't think an experienced thief would keep something so valuable as the Eye in so obvious a place. Darby, light that lamp would you, and bring it here."

Darby lit a kerosene lamp and handed it to Ming. The brothers crouched and studied the floorboards. Ming opened his pocket knife and began running it in the gaps between them. "Ah."

He picked up a small blue ceramic shard and held it between his thumb and forefinger. "When something as hard as ceramic shatters, pieces fly like shrapnel. So too terra cotta. Search around the edges of the floor."

Under a cabinet, Darby found a piece of terra cotta as long as his thumb, a piece of the warrior's arm. "How about this?"

The brothers studied it for a moment. "Excellent," said Hong. "Let us see whether there may be more."

"There is no time for this," said Chang. "In an hour it will be dawn."

"He is right," said Ming. "We don't want to be here in the daylight." He saw the pile of wood that had once been the crate. "The Tong dismantled the crate?"

Chang hesitated. "No, I did that. I thought there may be a hidden niche between the joints, but no. The boards are solid."

"Please have your men bring them to the mansion."

"What?"

"There may yet be something the crate can tell us." Hong took a purse from his pocket and poured out a handful of coins. "If this is not sufficient, there will be more later."

At that moment, the door burst open, and Chang's guards came in wrestling with a dark-clad figure, one of Meyung Loo's brotherhood. The struggle was fierce, but Chang ended it quickly by slamming the butt of his pistol down on the crown of the priest's head. The man's eyes rolled back in his head and he slumped forward.

"We found him outside," said one of the guards.

As he slipped to the floor, the sleeve of the Quang-Chi's tunic slid away, and the guards' eyes widened in surprise.

"This man is a priest," said Chang. "What is he doing here?"

"He has followed us," said Ming. "His order has engaged us to find the Eye for them. He followed us as a protector without our knowledge. We can take him with us. After all, it is bad luck to kill a priest."

Chang saw the looks on the faces of his men and smiled grimly, realizing Ming's strategy. Leave the decision to him, but plant the fear in his men if his choice is not Ming's will. "Very well, but know that this man owes you his life."

"His god will bless us all," said Hong. "Darby, please gather some of that mound of dust and put it in the satchel. That may have a story of its own."

"Min Li will see you back to your carriage." Chang looked around the room. "There are still things to be done here."

The brothers nodded and sidled out the door into the fog. Min Li said something in Mandarin to one of his fellows, and the thug heaved the priest over his shoulder. Darby was the last out the door.

Chang looked about the wreckage of the room and Won Lao's stolen goods. Nothing left that would fetch more than a few dollars. "Bundle the wood," he told his guard, and when Chen returns, send him for a cart."

He stared at the disemboweled corpse on the table. Was Won Lao a cog in the workings of this intricate intrigue, or was he simply a victim of blind chance? Either way, it no longer matters, he thought. The dead keep their own counsel.

Min Li returned and the three men carried the lumber from the crate into the alley where Chen waited with a mule cart. Chang said to Min Li. "Take the wood to the brothers, and come back at once."

The cart rattled off into the fog and Chang stepped back into the shanty. He took a coin from his pocket and placed it into Won Lao's mouth. Chang was not superstitious, but he was respectful. His eye drifted to the mound of excelsior pushed into a corner. He struck a match and threw it onto the pile. It flared into a bright yellow flame that licked at the walls.

"Join your ancestors."

By the time the flames shot through the roof of Won Lao's hovel, Chang was swallowed by the fog.

At the cry of "Fire!" the neighborhood woke and a bucket brigade passed water from a nearby pump and trough, but it was far too little and far too late. From an alleyway down the street, Feng Tao watched as Won Lao's shanty burned to the ground.

Too late, he thought. I learned his name too late, and I found his house too late. The Emperor will not be pleased.

XXXII

Taylor stopped the carriage at the gate. When he climbed down from the driver's seat, he said, "What about the priest? Do I leave him out here?"

"No," said Hong. "He needs attention. Bring him with us."

As the carriage pulled under the portico, Darby said, "I'll have nightmares for a week over that corpse. I need a drink."

"If you're going to drink, Darby, make it coffee. We will need your help."

Taylor lifted the unconscious priest in his arms and carried him up the steps onto the porch. The doors swung open and Raphael came out with a lamp in his hand.

"Put him on the divan in the parlor," said Hong. "Come with us, Darby, and bring the satchel."

Ming looked over his shoulder at the lightening sky. "As you said, brother, another interesting day."

They took the lift to the basement and went to the workroom that over the course of a few years had become a laboratory to rival those of many universities. The walls of the large, well-lit room were ringed with tables and cabinets, shelves of chemicals in stoppered glass bottles and flasks, pieces of exotic equipment, and bookcases filled with scientific texts.

"Put the satchel over there, please," said Ming. "And go upstairs and tell Raphael to make a pot of strong tea for us, and if you prefer, coffee for yourself. This will take some time."

Ming scooped out a measure of the powder and poured it into a petri dish. Beside him, Hong turned the terra cotta shard over in his fingers. "It looks very old," he said. "But is it?" He held the shard with a pair of forceps and with a small wire brush scraped a sample of the pale coating from the surface of the terra cotta into another dish. "Acid." He reached for a rubber apron hanging from a hook on the wall. It had two bibs and sets of shoulder straps. Ming reached behind with one of his hands, and Hong with one of his, and between them, they tied a neat, practiced bow in the apron string.

Ming nodded and the brothers wheeled toward a set of shelves lined with chemicals. Hong selected a bottle labeled H_2SO_4. He removed the stopper, careful to not inhale the fumes. He dipped the end of a glass rod into the acid and let the drop on its end fall into the dish. The reaction was immediate. The scrapings from the shard had crystallized.

Ming looked at the crystals in the dish with a magnifier. "We can run more tests for confirmation, but my immediate thought is calcium hydroxide."

"Yes, slaked lime. An old trick, but still effective to counterfeit antiquity."

"Like the terra cotta figures in the Morris collection."

"Yes. The statue was not generations old. The late Sing Chung lied to us."

"I'm shocked."

"As much as I," said Hong, shaking his head. "It appears that we were correct to refuse him."

"I also suspect that tests on the remains of the urn will find it too of recent manufacture."

"An elaborate scheme to smuggle the gem, but was it in either?"

"Perhaps, perhaps not."

Darby came in. "Chang's men are at the gate with the boards."

"Have them bring the wood to the side entrance," Ming said. "We would prefer to keep outsiders out of this room. You and Raphael can bring the wood down here."

Darby nodded and left.

"You are recalling Uncle Robert's lesson of the treasure box."

"Yes. It is a lesson that few learn."

One day when Ming and Hong were twelve years old, Uncle Robert came into their class room with a small metal box. It was the size of a deck of playing cards, painted green, and made of interlocking panels. He shook it, and something inside it rattled.

"This box holds a treasure," he said. "If you can open it, it will be yours."

The brothers took turns for the rest of the afternoon turning the box over in their hands, examining it from every angle and trying to press, pull and pry at the panels to no avail. Uncle Robert sat across the room in a chair by the window reading *Sonnets from the Portuguese*.

"Do you think that perhaps it cannot be opened?" whispered Hong, "that it somehow locks inside in some way that cannot be opened from the outside?"

"No," whispered Ming. "Uncle Robert has never given us a problem that can't be solved. There must be something you and I do not see."

"Both of us have tried every way we can think of and cannot open it."

"True," said Ming, "but we have been trying individually. Let us try the same methods together. Four hands can push and pull in ways that two hands cannot."

Ming pressed in on two of the sides while Hong pressed on the top, bottom and ends. The box remained closed. "Try pressing in combinations. Hong pressed the top then the bottom. No result. He pressed the top and each end in turn. Then he pressed the bottom and one end and felt something give ever so slightly. His eyes lit with excitement. He pressed on the bottom and the end again, this time pushing forward. When that didn't work, he pulled backward, and the top of the box slid back.

Inside was a piece of gravel from the driveway.

"That's no treasure," said Hong aloud. "It's just a piece of gravel. You said there was a treasure."

Uncle Robert set down his book and strolled over, his hands behind his back. "Have I ever deceived you?"

"Uh, no, sir. I meant no disrespect."

"The treasure is there. Your search is not over." He went back to his chair and picked up his book.

The brothers turned the opened box over in their hands and it looked no different than it had before. The winter sun slanted low when Uncle Robert finally set down his book. "Do you want me to show you the treasure?"

Ming and Hong looked at each other. They hated to admit defeat, but this time, they were stumped. "Yes, sir, said Ming. We would."

Uncle Robert adjusted his glasses on his nose and picked up the box in one hand and the stone in the other. He scraped the stone down the side of the box and the green paint came away, revealing the steel underneath. He repeated the process with the other sides, the bottom, and the lid. "Sometimes the treasure is inside the box and part of the box as well."

He scraped the bottom of the box with the stone, and a yellow gleam shone in the lamplight. The box was lined with gold. "It's like a 'smuggler's box,'" Uncle Robert said with a smile. Smugglers put a few trinkets in it, some cheap costume jewelry, and the customs inspector lets it pass with hardly a sniff, ignoring the true contraband.

"But the greatest treasure in the box is the lesson you have learned; two of them, in fact. One, take nothing for granted. Be thorough and explore all avenues. The other, what may not be solved by one, may be solved by both, if instead of competing; you work together toward the same end. Two heads are indeed better than one, if they share a common purpose."

Raphael and Darby came into the workroom, each with an armload of wood. "Set it over by the slop sink," said Ming. "And bring us brushes and kerosene."

"We must be thorough to be certain," said Ming.

"Perhaps the box is not just the box."

"We shall see."

Darby brought in a pair of tar-coated boards. "That's the last of them. Now what?"

Ming pointed to the hooks on the wall. "Get an apron."

Darby and the brothers scrubbed the tar from the boards one by one. The diluted tar filtered into the grain of the wood, making it more prominent. They set each plank in its turn on the work table and carefully examined it with a hand lens.

"I see something different in this plank," said Hong. Look at this end of the board, then look at the other"

Ming studied the ends of the plank carefully then nodded. "Yes. I see it too."

"See what?" said Darby, wiping his bleary eyes with his sleeve.

"No matter how clever the plan, someone always overlooks one small detail; in this case the difference between the saw cuts across the board. This end was cut with a much finer toothed saw than the others."

"So?"

"One end of this board was cut by laborers. The other was cut by a craftsman."

Inch by inch, the brothers probed the board, feeling for niches, and looking for seams. "Clever, clever," said Ming. "Our artisan has carved along the grain." He pressed at the section with his thumbnail and felt it give slightly. "He must have carved this with a scalpel. We have found one catch; let us look for others."

After more careful scrutiny, they found two more, each further apart from its mates than a human hand could span, requiring three people pressing in contradicting directions. They tried pressing them all at once to no effect.

"Try pressing and releasing at the same time," said Hong. "One, two three." Nothing happened.

"Now, let us try in sequence, Darby, then Hong, then myself."

Several tries later, Hong said, "Perhaps if one is held and another pressed and released, the third will open the chamber."

"Do you think it's in there?" said Darby, becoming exasperated.

Ming nodded. "I believe that it may be, yes."

"Then why don't you just split the board and save us all a lot of bother?"

"Because we cannot risk damaging the gem. Gems are brittle, and an errant blow from a hatchet could shatter one. Besides, if the Emperor's minions went to this much trouble to secrete the stone, they may well have set a trap for such as we; an explosive, a vial of poison, a nest of scorpions—who can say? Patience, Darby. Patience."

Hong said, "We can run through the set of sequences again, but this time the first person will hold the catch in while the others simply press and release." After exhausting those possibilities, he then said, "This time, the second person will hold his catch in while the others press and release."

Darby pressed his section and released it. Ming pressed his and maintained the pressure. Hong pressed his. There was a dull twang, and a chunk of wood carved so fine as to be undetectable popped from the board. An object wrapped in cloth and coated with wax lay in the recess.

"Is that it?" Darby pointed to the object.

"Patience, Darby." Ming probed gently under the cloth with the blade of his pocket knife. A sharp click, and four tiny needles jabbed into the recess, calculated to prick the finger of the unintended recipient. Ming reached into the recess and snapped off the delicate needles with his forceps. He held one close to its eye. "It is discolored. Poison." Then he gently took a corner of the cloth and lifted the object from its covert.

"Darby," said Hong, "please go to the third drawer in the white porcelain cabinet and bring me a scalpel."

While Ming held the waxed packet, Hong delicately cut at the cloth. When it parted, he peeled it away to reveal the blood red splendor of the Eye of Quang-Chi.

Darby whistled at the sight of the gem. "That's one hell of a jewel."

"Had Won Lao more time, he eventually would have found the Eye himself and be lying dead anyway," said Ming.

"Or the eye would be lying in the ashes of his stove," Hong replied.

"Should we inform Meyung Loo that we have found the gem?" said Ming.

"Let us not be too hasty. People have died for this stone. I think for now we should put it in the safe and collect ourselves before we hand it over."

"Are you having doubts about Meyung Loo, brother?"

"I am having doubts about this whole business. I have no doubt that Meyung Loo is genuine, and that his quest is real, but I wonder whether in giving him the Eye, we are signing his death warrant."

"If you're thinking about bringing in diplomatic help, I'm afraid Meyung wouldn't stand for it," Ming said. "He would no more trust Roger Summerlee than he would Sen Ti."

"And as a government official, Summerlee would be duty bound to report the matter to the authorities. The gem was smuggled into America, after all, and if found, it would be seized by Customs. Further, once Petterel got wind of it, the gem would be on its way to the Emperor."

"Sirs." Raphael stood in the doorway. "A message from Mister Foster at Oriental Trade."

The envelope held three sheets of foolscap written in the precise hand of Oriental Trade's Chief of Accounting and de facto manager. Ming held the letter and as he finished a page, passed it to Hong.

Darby waited, albeit impatiently, in silence.

Hong folded the letter. "Ambassador Sen Ti has been a busy fellow. He has sailed between San Francisco and Shanghai twice and once to Hong Kong, Sing Chung's city of origin, in the past four months. That puts him in place at the right times to have negotiated, if not the theft of the Eye, its transport to America by the Tong."

"And speaking of the Tong and how they could allow the crate to be stolen, the Parma Queen had calm waters and a swifter passage than usual. She docked a day and a half earlier than anticipated."

"Dumb luck," said Darby. "Just pure dumb luck."

"More people die from simple happenstance than all the conspiracies in the world," said Ming.

"I can speak only for myself, brother," said Hong. "But I need a bath and some sleep."

"I agree, but first, some breakfast or we will both starve to death. But before we sleep, there is one last thing we must do."

Upstairs in the parlor, they found their guest awake; face down on the floor with Raphael sitting on his shoulders, his neck in a choke hold. An angry red lump swelled over Raphael's left eye.

"He woke, sirs, and I was not going to allow him to leave without your permission."

"Did you tell him that?"

"I tried, sirs, but apparently my Chinese was not as good as I would have liked, nor his English."

"How long you been sitting like that?"

He looked at the clock on the mantel. "For about thirty-five minutes, sirs."

The brothers knelt beside them. Ming rapped his knuckles on the hardwood floor. The priest's eyes rolled toward him.

"Do you understand me?" Ming said in Mandarin.

"Yes." The priest was barely able to get the word out around Raphael's forearm.

"We need to speak with you. If our man releases his hold, you will not try to escape?"

"I will not."

Ming nodded and Raphael relaxed his grip on the man's throat but did not remove his arm.

"What is your name?"

"I am named Wu Sin."

"And you a priest of the Quang-Chi temple?"

"Yes."

"And Meyung Loo is your master?"

"Yes."

Hong broke in. "And are you a member of the Society of Righteous Fists?"

Wu Sin's eyes went wide. He bucked and tried to throw off Raphael, but the little man tightened his hold and in a few seconds, Wu Sin lay as they had found him.

"We are going to let you go now, said Ming. Please tell Meyung Loo we will meet with him here tomorrow at three o'clock to discuss the matter at hand." The brothers stepped away from the priest and once out of his immediate reach, nodded to Raphael, who sprang from his back as agile as a gymnast and as quickly had a pistol in his hand, but it was unnecessary. Wu Sin rose first to his knees, then he warily found his feet.

Raphael backed him into the foyer where Darby had opened the door. He gestured with the pistol and Wu Sin backed onto the porch. Down the driveway, the brothers saw Orville raising his rifle. Hong called. "It's all right, Orville. He was just leaving."

XXXIII

*I*n the afternoon , Ming and Hong stood once again staring at the chalkboard. They had added the deaths of Sing Chung and Won Lao, the location of the Eye in the crate, and the travels of Sen Ti.

"It is time to redraw the diagram," said Ming.

"I agree." Hong turned the board over and redrew the circles. In A, he wrote Sen Ti; in B, he wrote Meyung Loo, and in C he wrote Petterel. In the center, he wrote The Eye.

"Motive," said Ming, picking up his chalk.

Under Meyung Loo's name, he wrote "faith."

Under Sen Ti's name, he wrote "power."

"What to write under Petterel's name?"

"One of the three most common: survival, lust, or greed."

Ming nodded and wrote "greed" in C.

"I am not sure whether faith is Meyung's sole motive," said Hong. "His desire to find the Eye goes beyond restoring an icon to his temple. He opposes the Emperor." He wrote "politics" in the intersection between A and B. In the sector between B and C he wrote "official opposition".

"Is Petterel's hand on his own tiller, or might he be taking orders from a higher authority?"

"The Mayor? The Governor?" Hong shook his head. "Darby uncovered links between Petterel and Sing, but not between him and Collins. As for Sacramento, I could not say, although little happens in California that is unknown to the Governor and his minions. Perhaps Darby will find a link in his research today."

Ming drew a dollar sign in the intersection between A and C. "And money drives the whole infernal machine. Tammany Ring has nothing on Sacramento."

"The information on Sen Li suggests that he instrumental in this whole scheme, if not its architect."

"The Emperor's power has dwindled since the Sino-Japanese War. Such concern over a small corner of his empire raises the question; do the Quang-Chi brothers have another affiliation?"

"The Society of Righteous Fists?"

"Yes," said Ming. "The Boxers. They become more powerful every season and they are a true threat to the Emperor."

"That is a question we must ask Meyung Loo when we next meet."

"The sale of the Eye would buy many rifles."

"Wheels within wheels."

The gate bell rang. On the street, a hansom stood, the driver waiting by the bell. Raphael spoke to him through the gate and unlocked it. He stepped back, pulling the gate open, and as the cab rolled past him, he bowed.

Both brothers smiled. There was only one person whom Raphael would admit without consulting them first: Maria.

Raphael was taking her coat when the lift arrived in the foyer. "Maria, what a surprise," said Hong.

"A lovely surprise," Ming amended. "And you look lovely."

Maria blushed and demurely looked down at her blue satin dress. In her arms she carried a large leather folio.

"Please, come into the parlor," said Ming, offering her his arm.

"Raphael, please bring tea," said Hong.

"Very good, sirs."

Maria arranged her skirts and bustle in a tufted velvet armchair, and the brothers sat facing her on a divan. No one spoke for a minute, and in the awkward silence, Maria sat, hands folded, staring into her lap. Finally, she spoke.

"Ming, Hong, I owe you both an apology. I had no right to speak to you as I did the other night. You have both been so gracious and supportive. I behaved like a petulant child, and I am sorry. Please forgive me."

"There is nothing to forgive, Maria. You spoke your heart, and you are free to do so always."

Hong added, "The night was a very difficult time. You were in shock from what happened. No forgiveness is necessary." Diplomatically changing the subject, he said, "What is in the folio you brought with you?"

"Part of a favor I would ask. The Opera House has been closed for several days, and I have nowhere to rehearse. I fear that if I don't sing, my voice will suffer. Would you be so kind as to accompany me?"

The brothers beamed. "It would be our pleasure," said Hong.

Raphael wheeled the tea cart into the parlor. "Raphael," said Ming, "please bring the tea to the music room."

"Very good, sirs."

"Come, my dear," said Ming, "and let us whisk you away in our brazen car."

She laughed, and the brothers realized that they were forgiven too.

Maria's folio held a variety of scores. "What would you like to sing first?" Ming said.

"Perhaps the Vivaldi, after I do my warm up exercises."

Maria sang scales *a capella*, then some *solfeggio* exercises, acclimating her voice to the acoustics of the room and its resonant tones. Finally, she let her voice ring out in its full glory, filling the music room with sweet reverberation.

Ming set the Vivaldi score on the piano, *"Alla caccia d'un bello adorato"*.
"Shall we flip a coin to see who plays first?" Ming jibed.

"No need," said Hong, "You play the left hand, and I'll play the right."

The brothers nodded to sync each other to the tempo, . . . five, six, seven,
eight. The orchestral introduction was artfully reduced to a piano score so
that in the smaller space on the grand piano, it sounded no less full. Their
fingers lovingly caressed the keys of the piano, coaxing emotion from
ivory and ebony.

Maria began so sing; a fount of beauty poured from her heart, filling
the room and filling the brothers' souls with its gentle force. Their breath
quickened and their shared heart seemed to pulse with the music, and in
time with Maria's own. Ming and Hong had played the score often before,
as they had so many, but never had they done so with such feeling.

Maria felt it too as their music swirled around the room, filling its every
corner with its throbbing, by turns haunting, seductive, and forceful.
Ming and Hong each stole a look at Maria, whose eyes met their own each
in turn with a deep gaze that left them breathless. Their breath quickened.
Another's fingers might have fumbled at the keys, but the brothers' hands
played almost instinctively, coaxing the soul from every note as their
bodies moved with the rhythm and the rush of blood flushed their faces
and roared in their ears.

The aria ended with a high piercing note that entered the brothers' ears
and shot through them like an electric current, wrapping them in a cold
fire so potent that they almost couldn't play the last four measures. Maria's
bosom rose and fell in a long shuddering sigh. The three stared at each
other in stunned silence. There were no words to be said.

The gate bell rang, breaking the spell. Maria blinked as if waking from
a trance.

The brothers had composed themselves by the time Raphael arrived to
announce the visitor, but just barely.

"Sirs, Detective Harmon is at the gate with several officers and a search
warrant."

XXXIV

"Raphael, bring pen and paper." Hong pulled his watch from his pocket.
"Judge Werther may be home by now."

"Let us hope so," said Ming.

Maria's eyed darted between them in confusion. "I don't understand. What do the police want?"

"To keep us from doing our job," Ming said, as Hong quickly dashed off a letter, signed it, and handed Ming the pen. "Raphael, take this to Judge Werther as quickly as possible, and tell him the matter is urgent."

Raphael barely got "Yes, sirs" out of his mouth before he was through the doorway and headed for the stairs.

Hong rang for Taylor. "We need a presence at the gate. Taylor may have more effect than Raphael."

"Please stay here, my dear," said Ming squeezing Maria's hand. The brothers took the lift to the second floor. From the office window, Hong counted six uniforms plus an impatiently pacing Harmon. From the window at the end of the hall they saw two more at the rear gate. "Nine of them."

"Far too many for us to watch all at once. Who knows what mischief they may do?"

"And if they find the safe, we will be obligated to open it, or they will open it themselves and find the Eye."

"If Raphael is quick enough, they will not have the opportunity."

Downstairs, the brothers opened the double doors and stepped onto the front porch. Taylor was waiting with a .10 gauge shotgun, stock against his hip. "Please accompany us, and shoot only if we are in peril."

The brothers strolled casually down the driveway, taking their time, stopping to look at one thing or another. "Stop stalling," shouted Harmon. "I have a warrant."

Ming smiled and waved to Harmon as if he'd said a greeting instead. They continued their leisurely pace. When they reached the gate, the brothers saw two of the officers holding sledge hammers. Harmon was prepared to force their entry.

"Good afternoon, Detective," said Hong. "Raphael tells us that you have a warrant." His inflection rose at the end of the sentence, making it a question.

"You're damned right I do." He held up a folded paper. I have a warrant to search the house and grounds. Open the gate. Now!"

"May we see it, please?" Hong reached his hand through the bars of the gate.

Harmon snapped, "You can read it while we search the place. Open the gate."

Hong turned his head. "Brother, do you have the key?"

"Raphael, take this to Judge Werther."

Ming shook his head. "I do not. Taylor, do you have the key?" The big man shook his head, never taking his eyes off the one officer whose hand was slowly moving toward his pistol. As subtly, Taylor brought the shotgun to waist level and curled his finger around the triggers.

"We will have to return to the house for it," said Hong. "I apologize for the inconvenience."

An angry flush was creeping from Harmon's celluloid collar to his cheeks. "Don't bother. We brought our own key." He gestured with his head toward the men with the hammers.

"As you wish," said Ming, "but I would inform you that the lock is German made, designed for prisons, and built to withstand a charge of dynamite."

Harmon looked ready to explode himself at the flaunting of his authority in front of his men. He turned to the pair with the sledges. "Break it open."

The coppers stepped forward and Harmon stepped back.

"This is all unnecessary," said Ming. "As I said, we will go for the key."

"You'll stay right where you are," snarled Harmon. He nodded to the officers, and the assault on the gate began. Like gandydancers driving rail spikes, the pair worked in rhythm, pounding the square of the lock. Two minutes later, they had succeeded only in tiring themselves. The lock was barely dented.

An officer the brothers recognized as one of Hawkins' crew from the opera house stepped forward and drew his pistol and pointed at the brothers. "All right, that's it. No more stalling. Open the gate."

Taylor turned slightly bringing the bore of the shotgun where its aim would do the most damage.

"Jenks, what are you doing?" Harmon said. "Put that gun away."

"Shut up, Harmon." then to the brothers, "Did you hear me? I said open the gate now."

The silence that followed was broken only by the click of the shotgun's hammers as Taylor's thumb pulled them back. The other officers drew their pistols, uncertain. Ming looked over his shoulder to the house and saw Maria at the office window. He prayed for her sake, not his that she would not have to watch them die.

Jenks said, "There are seven of us. You can't kill us all."

"Only most of you," said Taylor unmoving.

"What are you men doing here?" The voice came from behind the policemen. A tall man in a frock coat with long sideburns that grew into his thick grey moustache stood, arms akimbo, with Raphael beside him.

"Good day, sir," said Ming. "The Detective is rather insistent about serving a warrant."

Harmon's mouth opened but nothing came out of it, for a second, then he croaked, "Judge Werther." The officers parted like the Red Sea before the Honorable Judge Hiram Q. Werther, who plucked the warrant from Harmon's fingers. Behind him, Jenks' eyes glittered, sensing an advantage. Taylor would not fire the shotgun; he might hit the Judge. Taylor locked eyes with Jenks and said quietly, "Don't fool yourself."

Werther scanned the document. "Who signed this drivel?" he boomed. "Compton. I should have known." He said to the dumbfounded Harmon, "Turn around."

"Uh, what, sir?"

"I said turn around, Detective. Are you deaf *and* stupid?" Harmon turned his back to the judge, who used it as a writing desk. He pulled a gold fountain pen from an inside pocket and scrawled something across the face of the warrant. "Take these men and leave, Detective."

"Judge, this is a murder investigation. I have a warrant."

"Which I have just officially quashed. As a Federal District judge, my authority exceeds Compton's by about twenty leagues. Next time you ask for a warrant, Detective, make sure you have probable cause. Now apologize to these people and go home. And if you harass these men in this fashion again, you'll be violating a Federal court order, and I'll see you sent to Alcatraz."

Harmon turned to his men. "All right, back to the wagon." All of them complied, except for Jenks, who tarried a moment, staring down Taylor and still pointing his revolver. He backed away and kept Taylor's eye until he disappeared around the corner.

Once the police were gone, Werther said, "Now, will someone please tell me what the hell is going on here?"

XXXV

They sat in the parlor, Ming and Hong and the Judge, and over cigars and brandy the brothers told him the story of the Eye and all of the intrigue that surrounded it, excluding details that would warrant prosecution of themselves or their agents.

When they told of Petterel's relationship with the Ambassador, Ming said, "The two of them are in this to the hilt, although we can't see all around it yet. I am sure Harmon's warrant was at Petterel's instigation. He wants us out of this matter. He and Sen Ti both deserve prison, at the least, and we'd like to put them there."

"You'll have the Devil's own time jailing Sen Ti. His diplomatic immunity covers a multitude of sins. Petterel's a different story, and he's a bad one," said the Judge. "Has been since I was a County Judge and he was a prosecutor. But he's also connected to some high powered people, and he's as slippery as they come. He'll have a cold chair in hell, that one."

"It's good that you came when you did," said Hong. "We are very grateful."

Werther chuckled. "Just being a good neighbor. Besides, I've known you boys since you were in knee pants. Your father was a fine man and a good friend. I could do no less."

Hong said to Ming, "Our gate impervious to dynamite? That was quick thinking, brother."

"But another minute or so with the hammers and the ruse would have been disproven. Again, fortune was with us that Jenks drew his pistol when he did."

"Yes, Jenks," said Hong. "He is one of Petterel's private enforcers. "Harmon seemed as surprised as we that he suddenly took command. That makes me think that Harmon was just a pawn in this gambit. Jenks apparently had orders to get into the mansion by any means."

"Two attempts on your lives and now this, all in a week." said Werther. He took a long draw on his cigar. "Apparently Petterel finds the two of you a threat, or maybe Sen Ti does and he's pulling Petterel's strings. In any case, if I can help you I will."

"We would not want to compromise you in any way, Judge," said Hong.

"Hell, I wouldn't see the inside of a jail cell if I cut Grover Cleveland's throat on Market Street on the Fourth of July."

"Your offer is most generous," said Ming, "and we will keep it in mind as things unfold."

Music drifted from upstairs. The rich sound of the grand piano underlay Maria's sweet voice as she sang softly, a love song in French.

The Judge's eyebrows raised. "You have company other than myself."

"Yes," said Hong smiling. "Miss Donatelli was rehearsing in our music room when the police arrived.

"Well," said Werther," I will take my leave now so that you may return to your guest."

"Thank you again for your intervention. Shall we have Taylor escort you to your home?"

"It's a short walk," Werther said, "and the day I skulk around in fear of piss ants like that bunch, it's time to resign. Good evening, gentlemen."

Upstairs, Maria sat at the piano. She rose from the bench and put an arm around each of the brother's necks and held them close. "I was so afraid," she said. "But I was proud of you too, the way you stood up to those men."

"We had a little help. Taylor is a great deterrent to violence. And if the Judge hadn't arrived when he did, the story may have had a different ending."

"But he came because you thought quickly and acted boldly. That is worthy of itself." She kissed Ming on his cheek and Hong on his. "I should go."

"Yes," said Hong, "you should, but not for the reasons you think. We are in a precarious position at the moment, and the last thing that we wish is to have you harmed by it in any way."

"I agree," said Ming. "We will have Taylor drive you home." He smiled. "But there will be other days, Maria."

She blushed and looked away, embarrassed, then she turned back to the brothers and smiled, firm in her resolve. "Yes. There will be many, many days. I am sure of it."

XXXVI

*D*arby returned just before supper. "You'll be happy to know that I have some news," he said. "I was at the Public Library going through the newspaper archives. I'm coming out when somebody taps me on the shoulder. It's my friend Bill MacInerny, one of my sources in the Leyden Shipping Investigation. He tells me, 'You're gonna want to hear what I heard yesterday.'

"I hand him a five, and he says, 'Hit me again.' I do, and he tells me Leyden Shipping has a buyer, someone called Empire Transport."

"I've never heard of them," said Ming.

"Nor I," said Hong.

"Me either," said Darby. "So I turn around and go right back into the library. It took a while, but I found out Empire Transport is a San Francisco concern. That led me to City Hall and the public records for DBA names. You'll never guess who the Chairman of the Board of Directors is." He paused dramatically. "Robert Victor Hawkins. Sergeant Robert Victor Hawkins."

"Petterel's bulldog," said Ming. "He is just one big muscle. He knows as much about running a shipping line as a cypress stump might. He's just a front for Petterel."

"And that's not all," Darby said. "The Secretary Treasurer is a man named Mi Ho. He is an employee of the Chinese Mission. He is an aide to Sen Ti."

"Excellent work," said Ming.

"Now the circle closes," said Hong.

"And that, gentlemen, is why you keep me on the payroll."

"It is time to revisit the diagram," said Ming.

"What a twisted story," said Darby. "It almost makes me wish I was a reporter again so I could write it up. A headline and a byline."

"Why settle for reporting history, Darby, when you can shape its events instead? Let us see what Raphael has prepared for this evening."

XXXVII

Sen Ti's valet packed his clothing carefully into the steamer trunk. In six hours, the Ambassador would leave his hotel and board a ship to Shanghai. The mission did not go as he would have liked, but there were other men who would be happy to partner with one such as he. Petterel would have been ideal. The Commissioner could have kept law enforcement at bay while Sen Li's people smuggled opium and women into the country by the ship load.

Another thorn, Meyung Loo still lived, and the priest would continue to be a source of irritation as long as he did. Sen had planned for him to be killed in America and forgotten in his homeland, but that too did not turn out as planned. But he would never find the Eye of Quang-Chi. Sen had made certain of that.

In some ways, it was fortunate for him that the crate was stolen. He could keep the eye and the Emperor's loss would be blamed on the Tong.

In the meantime, the sale of the eye would finance the purchase of Oriental Trading with another hidden partner.

There was a knock at the door to his suite. Sen heard his valet answer it. Too early for the porter to pick up the trunk, he thought. Then he heard a strangled scream from the next room. Sen Ti slammed the bedchamber door and turned the key. He grabbed the strap of his diplomatic pouch and slung it over his shoulder. He turned the knob of the door to the hallway and it burst inward, knocking him back and onto the bed.

A Chinaman in a long coat and a slouch hat pressed a gun against Sen Li's forehead. The door to the adjacent room swung in with a sharp crack, and Ching Toy strode into the room.

"What is the meaning of this?" said Sen Ti, with as much threat as he could muster.

"You dare to ask," said Ching, "when you were the architect of this whole charade?"

"You dare to put your hands on me, to accuse me."

"I will do more." Ching struck Sen Li with the back of his hand and nearly knocked him off the bed. "Where is the Eye, deceiver?"

"I do not have it." Sen Ti wiped a trickle of blood from the corner of his mouth.

"Who else then? You made fools of us all, chasing each other, each thinking the other had it, and all along it was nestled in your sack." Ching drew his knife and held to Sen Ti's throat. "Is it in there now?"

Ching's man ripped the pouch from Sen Ti's shoulder and dumped its contents onto the bed. Papers slithered every direction, and on top of them a leather drawstring pouch landed with a thump. Ching held the pouch in front of the Ambassador's eyes. "Is it in here, deceiver?"

Ching turned the pouch sideways and a flood of rubies poured into his palm. "Explain."

"Yes, I brought the Eye in my pouch. I had it cut under the Emperor's instructions to be sold and scattered to the four winds, to destroy that accursed religious sect. You can ask Feng Tao. He is the Emperor's emissary. We all do the Emperor's will. He will tell you."

"I think not," said Ching. He motioned with his head to the next room. A third Tong came in carrying a stained burlap bag. He dumped the sack and Feng Tao's head rolled across the floor, stopping on its side, as if he were listening to something underneath the carpet.

"You were paid," said Sen.

"Not nearly enough. My cousin died pursuing this fool's quest." Ching funneled the rubies back into the pouch with his palm. "These will go in some small measure to repay his family."

"You cannot!" shouted Sen Li. "Those stones belong to the Emperor. You cannot betray the Emperor!"

"This is America, deceiver. We have no Emperor." With one slash, Ching opened Sen's artery, with a second, his vein.

Sen clutched vainly at his throat but found that holding back his blood was like holding back the sea.

XXXVIII

Supper was excellent. Raphael had prepared rack of lamb in a brandy sauce with green beans julienne and candied yams. Darby ate as much as Ming and Hong together. After the meal, the three sat in the parlor with cigars and whiskey.

"One thing puzzles me," said Darby. "Why the sudden rash of attempts on your life? Two in just a few days? Was that part of this business about the Eye?"

"The priests are men of some influence, and if we are correct that they have ties to the Righteous Fists, the Boxers, they have more backing than we were led to believe, including the Boxers' network of intelligence. So, finding the thief and tracing his steps was easier in their own land. They knew the jewel left the country on a ship bound for San Francisco. Once they arrived here, they soon found that they were not up for the task."

"At the risk of sounding egotistical, when they made enquiries as to who in this city would be most likely to find a needle in this giant haystack, our names were mentioned," said Ming. "I have no doubt that they are watched from the shadows, and their intention to consult us was known before Meyung ever rang the bell. When word got out that the crate was stolen and the Eye was somewhere at large in the city, Sen Ti pressured Petterel to make sure no one else found the Eye. Having us killed was one path to that end, to stop the Quang-Chi priests."

"That explains the American killers. Petterel's choices to take attention away from the Tong," Darby said. "Petterel's been in this play from the outset."

"And between him and Sen Ti, a shipping line could have almost unlimited freedom to bring any contraband between Shanghai and San

Francisco, with influence at either destination to prevent detection. I am beginning to question whether the Emperor sanctioned this gambit at all or perhaps Sen Ti was running his own game to make himself richer than he already is"

"And he and Petterel were old friends already. Who better to partner in a smuggling scheme on so grand a scale than the Police Commissioner?"

"The evil bastards," said Darby. "So how do we get them?"

"That," said Ming, "is a question for which we as yet have no answer."

XL

The clock in the Custom House tower struck four. In the shadows, a group of men, a dozen or more, slipped on black hoods. They checked their guns and readied themselves without saying a word. Their leader waved a silent signal, and they spread in twos and threes to different streets and alleyways, keeping to the shadows, all to converge on one place: the Smith mansion.

Under his mask, Hawkins smiled without mirth. Petterel and his slant-eyed partner thought they were so clever setting up their scheme. But in the end, he thought, it always comes down to lead and steel, something for which neither Petterel nor Sen Li had the stomach. But Hawkins did, and once the smart boys had their operation up and running, it was lead and steel that would take it from them and make Hawkins a rich and powerful man. But first, the Smiths.

The fog was light tonight, almost none at all; bad luck for them. A half moon shone pale light on the cobble stoned pavement. Not the best conditions, thought Hawkins, but good enough.

His men rounded the corner and saw a block away the roof lines of the mansions on Angle Street. Any one of them cost more than a cop like him could earn in a lifetime, but soon enough, he'd have his pick of the lot.

Hawkins and his men slipped into their position directly opposite the front gate. Jenks had the men at the rear. The windows of the mansion were dark. The Smiths and their men would be snug in their beds. If they had a sentry, one man wouldn't last long against fifteen trained gunmen.

He would lead the frontal assault once the gate was open, and his men would converge from all sides to take the mansion quickly and efficiently. Hawkins felt a thrill in his gut he hadn't felt since Gettysburg. He checked his watch. It was time.

At the back gate, Jenks tried one key, then another, then another until he found the one that opened the lock. He and four others slipped through into the garden.

On the roof, Tom heard the creak of the hinge. He strained his eyes to see the garden below and saw the dark shapes of men moving through the corridor of arbor vitae toward the house. Tom thumbed back the hammer of his Henry and took aim at the leader. Fish in a barrel.

From a block away, a man in a suit and a derby hat moved from streetlamp to streetlamp in full view. He was carrying a small satchel and hurrying as if on urgent business. The man was Gallagher, the watch corporal from the precinct station. He reached the Smiths' gate and pulled the bell cord.

Hawkins said one word under his breath to his men: "Ready."

Gallagher waited a moment and pulled the bell cord again. A light came on in the first floor. He set the satchel by the gate and reached into his coat pocket for a cigar. He casually wet it between his lips and struck a match on the stone of the gate pillar. He lit the cigar and puffed out a cloud of smoke and blew out the match.

Then he bent at the waist as if reaching into the satchel and lit the fuse to the dynamite.

Gallagher spun on his heel and ran, but not fast enough. Both barrels of Orville's shotgun roared as he fired through the bars of the gate, and Gallagher separated into two halves in a dark spray of blood.

One second later, the dynamite went off.

XLI

Raphael was halfway down the drive to answer the bell when a bright yellow flash and a roar erupted at the gate. The concussion knocked him backward, almost off his feet. The blast twisted the wrought iron gate like taffy, and it hung from one hinge to the side. Through the acrid smoke, he saw masked men rushing across the street firing guns and his only thought was to protect the brothers.

He drew a pistol from his waistband and returned their fire until the hammer clicked on empty cylinders. He was almost at the porch when a shot hit him like a giant fist and knocked him on his face. His last conscious thought was "bar the door."

At the sound of Orville's shotgun, Tom squeezed off his first shot. A scream let him know he'd hit his target. Before he could lever another round into the chamber, the explosion at the gate knocked him almost over the ornate iron fence of the widow's walk on the roof of the tower. He dragged himself back over the railing as return fire whanged off the wrought iron spears.

Orville threw down the empty shotgun and picked up his Winchester. He fired into the crowd of invaders as fast as he could work the lever and saw at least two of the masked men fall, but there looked to be at least ten of them, and he had to duck behind a tree as they fired a fusillade of shots at him. Two of them had him pinned down while the others ran toward the house.

Chunks of the tree stung Orville's face as bullets ripped through it. He rolled to the side and came up firing, hitting one of the pair. The man dropped his rifle and staggered forward drawing a revolver. Before it cleared the holster, a dark shape leapt from the shadows and wrapped itself around him, the Quang-Chi priest.

The priest drew a blade across the gunman's throat as his partner fired a shot that caught the priest just above his shoulder. The priest tried to stand, and his head lolled on half a neck. A second shot, and the priest lay still.

On the roof, Tom lit a kerosene lantern, cranked up the flame, and threw it from the roof onto the garden path. The lantern burst and in seconds, the arbor vitae caught fire. In the yellow glow he saw two men trapped between rows of burning bushes. One of them beating out flames from a splash of kerosene on his clothes. Nowhere to run, you bastards, he thought, and pulled the trigger.

Hawkins and his men ran up the drive. The gravel crunched under their boots, but they couldn't hear it because of the ringing in their ears. They were almost at the portico when Taylor burst through the front door, a pistol blazing in each hand. Hawkins' men scattered for cover.

Upstairs, Darby came running, barefoot in his trousers and undershirt, the .410 pistol in one hand and his Derringer in the other. Ming and Hong were pulling on their trousers.

"Somebody's blown the gate," said Darby. "There are gunmen all over the place. Stay here. I'll guard the stairs."

"No, said Hong. This is our home. Go downstairs. We'll take the lift."

"This will be over soon. The cops will be here any minute."

"I don't think Petterel will allow that to happen." Hong picked up his pistol from the night stand. Go downstairs."

Tom picked off the burning man easily enough, but his partner dove through the burning arbor vitae and fired from the darkness behind.

On the back porch, Jenks turned Darby's key and the door swung inward on quiet hinges. He stepped into the dark hallway and carefully picked his way toward the glow of light from the front of the mansion. He heard gunfire and the crackle of flames, men shouting, and something else. The hum of machinery. The lift. Monkeys in a cage.

Outside Hawkins and his men traded shots with Taylor. Hawkins signaled one of his men to circle around to try to catch the coachman from the side. They men laid down cover fire for him, and he slipped through the lilac trees toward the side of the portico. Where is he?

Taylor's pistol blazed and the gunman got a fix on his target. He aimed his rifle where he thought Taylor's bulk would be. One more shot, you son of a bitch, he thought, and I'll have you.

A burst of pain exploded in his back and the gunman jerked the trigger, sending the shot wild over Taylor's head. Raphael twisted the knife as the masked man clawed desperately behind him. The Honduran drew out the knife and plunged it in again and again until the gunman lay still. A bullet whistled through the branches. Taylor was shooting back. Raphael picked up the dead man's rifle with his good hand and crawled back the way he came.

Taylor paused to reload and saw a dim shape creeping around the edge of the porch. The shadow stood up, but before it could fire, Taylor swung the cut-down Winchester that hung from a thong in his armpit up and fired three quick rounds. The shadow fell backwards into the brush with a crash.

Taylor wiped blood from his forehead. One of the shots had grazed him, but not done as much damage as it might have.

On the roof, Tom realized that he was now at a disadvantage. He had an idea where the gunman was in the garden below, but the glare of the firelight made it difficult for him to see anywhere but the path. Every time he moved for a shot, a bullet hit the widow's walk. Sooner or later, his adversary was going get lucky. The tower was eight feet above the attic. The pitch of the roof was steep, and from the eave, it was another ten or twelve feet to the shallow roof over the back porch. Then ten feet or so to the garden.

Tom raised his head and a bullet ricocheted off the railing. He saw the flash from the rifle and knew where the sniper was hiding, a wooded nook beside the fountain. He drew his Colt from its holster and tied a lanyard to the ring in it butt. Gripping the pistol, he launched himself over the railing and raced down the slate tiles feet first like a boy on a bobsled.

Tom tried to slow himself by spragging his heels, but the tiles were too smooth. He was going too fast to control his fall. He flew over the eave and landed hard on the porch roof, rolling too fast to stop. He tried to tuck and roll when he hit the garden, but his leg twisted under him and he heard it crack as pain shot through him.

He was lucky. He had landed behind the sniper and taken him completely by surprise. The masked man turned, not two feet from Tom, and before he could swing his rifle, Tom emptied his Colt into the mask. The man fell backward into the fountain, and as Tom dragged himself to his feet, he saw the water of the fountain turn red in the pale moonlight.

Tom dragged himself to a marble love seat, sank onto it, and promptly passed out.

The lift passed the second floor. The gunfire was louder now, echoing upward from the front of the house. "I'll never laugh at you again for carrying a gun," said Ming.

"In a moment, we'll both have one."

In the foyer, Jenks watched as the bottom of the brass elevator car slowly descended. In a minute, he thought, I'll put an end to this.

Hawkins was down to three men at the front. He should have run for it, but the blood lust raged through him and its imperative wouldn't allow a retreat. Where the hell was Jenks?

Up the street, a fire wagon came to a halt, its bells clanging. Angle Street was blocked by a police wagon and a handful of uniformed officers.

"We have to get through. There's a fire."

"There's a situation going on down there, gunfire and explosions. You can't go in until it's over."

The Chief fumed, but had no choice other than wait for permission to do his job.

The bottom of the lift appeared. Jenks smiled. As the gleaming brass framework descended, he saw feet, shins, knees. He raised his rifle. Waists. He blinked at the sight of the brothers' bare torsos and the thick trunk of flesh and bone that joined them. Their faces came into view, startled eyes staring, and Jenks opened fire.

The brothers fell to the floor of the car as bullets ricocheted around them. Hong fired his pistol between the brass slats and Jenks ducked, but continued to fire.

"Like monkeys in a cage you slant-eyed freaks." He stepped closer and took aim through the brass lattice.

At the same second the brothers heard a roar, Jenks flew upward sideways like a hooked trout yanked from a stream. He crashed into the wall and lay still. Hong reached up and stopped the lift. Darby was picking himself up from the floor.

"I fired both barrels," he said. "Good thing I came down the back stairs, or he'd've gotten us all."

Hawkins and his men were taking turns firing and reloading when a voice from behind them said, "Hey, boys." They wheeled to find Orville and Raphael holding them at gunpoint. One of Hawkins' men tried to get off a shot, but Orville's Winchester punched a hole in his chest. Hawkins stared down at his empty revolver.

"Don't shoot him," Taylor said, stepping into view from the portico. "This bird's mine."

"Yeah," spat Hawkins. "Go on and shoot an unarmed man. That's your style, you fucking ape."

Taylor put his revolvers in their holsters and unbuckled the rig. He let the pistols drop to the ground. He reached behind his back and pulled out a bowie knife. He pointed to the sheath hanging from Hawkins' belt. "You've got one. Let's see how you use it."

Hawkins stood and pulled his weapon, a wicked foot-long blade more like a short saber than a knife, with a brass knuckle grip. He pulled off his hood and threw it aside. The sergeant drew the blade across the back of his forearm and held it up as blood dripped from his elbow. "Nothing to fear." He stepped under the portico and sneered, "Have at it, boyo." The men circled each other, each watching for an opening. Hawkins was a good six inches taller than Taylor and had a longer reach, so Taylor kept his distance.

"Come on, you woman," spat Hawkins. "You fight like your sister."

Taylor moved with surprising speed for a man of his size and build and the tip of his knife slit open Hawkins' shirt an inch above his navel. Hawkins danced backward, knocking Taylor's knife hand away and aimed a kick at Taylor's groin. Taylor twisted to the side and Hawkins' boot hit his hip with the force of a sledge hammer, numbing his leg.

Taylor kept his left forearm up as he circled Hawkins. Blood was seeping through the slit in Hawkins' shirt and Taylor could tell by the amount that the cut wasn't deep enough to do substantial damage.

Hawkins parried over Taylor's forearm, jabbing at his eye with the tip of his blade. Taylor's head snapped back, and as Hawkins pulled back the knife, he twisted his hand and made a backhand slash to Taylor's bicep.

Taylor swung his knife from the outside, but Hawkins blocked him with a two-by-four wrist. Taylor's foot lashed out and caught Hawkins' knee. The sergeant grunted in pain and danced back out of Taylor's reach, swinging his blade in a tight figure eight. He was favoring the knee now, and Taylor had put him in a defensive posture. He backed around, swinging his blade and daring Taylor to step into reach. Taylor circled him clockwise to make him pivot on the damaged knee. He could see the grimace of pain on Hawkins' face.

Taylor tried a sideways maneuver, but Hawkins was too quick for him. Taylor realized that his only chance was to risk his arm. Cutting figure eights in the air, Hawkins would lose a precious second to cock his wrist to thrust. Taylor feinted with his blade and when Hawkins turned to block it, Taylor drove his fist through a loop of the figure eight and caught Hawkins on the side of his jaw.

The sergeant's head snapped back, but he didn't fall, and Taylor drew his fist away bloody from the edge of Hawkins' blade. "You got to do better than that, boy," Hawkins hissed. He slashed with his saber and Taylor blocked it with his knife. Sparks flew as the blades struck each other, and Taylor caught Hawkins' blade guard to guard. They struggled that way for a moment, and Hawkins caught Taylor with a gut punch that lifted him off the ground.

Taylor spun to the side and rolled away an instant before Hawkins' boot heel crashed where his head had been. Taylor raised into a crouch, favoring his side. He couldn't let Hawkins get him on the ground, or he'd be finished. Hawkins rushed at him arms wide, and Taylor threw himself to the side, slashing Hawkins' leg as he did. In a second, Taylor was on his feet, his breath ragged. His knife hand hung at his side, the handle loose in his fingers.

Hawkins grinned and held the saber in front of his face in a mock salute. "This is how it ends, lad. Your friends may kill me, but you'll be in hell when I get there." Hawkins took a step forward and Taylor's arm snapped up, throwing the Bowie knife underhand. It pierced Hawkins' gut and before he could pull it out, Taylor ducked under Hawkins' arms and threw his shoulder into the handle, driving it through him and out his back.

Hawkins staggered backward, stunned by pain and surprise. His saber dangled from the knuckle grip. Taylor wrenched it from his hand and

"You got one. Let's see how you use it."

both of his own rammed the point upward through the flesh of Hawkins' throat, skewering his tongue and piercing his palate into his skull.

Taylor let go of the knife and Hawkins fell backward, twitched for a few seconds then lay still.

Ming and Hong, each holding a shotgun, stood on the porch beside Darby.

"Do you want us to kill these two?" said Orville.

"No," said Ming. "Step away from them." Orville and Raphael looked at each other and did as they were told.

"You men come into our home in the dead of night to kill us in our beds. Animals. We, however, are civilized men. Pick up your guns."

"What the hell are you doing?" said Darby.

"Giving them the chance they would not have given us. As I said, we are civilized men." Ming pointed his shotgun at the ground and his brother followed suit.

Darby stepped away from the brothers and said to the two masked gunmen. "You heard the man."

The invaders looked at each other, and at their pistols lying on the ground. Both dived at once, scooping up their guns as one rolled left and one rolled right. The one to the left, whom Raphael had shot in the shoulder, got off one round, and the one to the right fired twice before the twin shotguns cut them to pieces.

Darby touched Hong's ear. "You're bleeding."

"Yes. He shot us," said Hong. "I believe that makes it self-defense."

"Where is Tom?"

"I don't know," said Orville. I haven't heard gunfire from the widow's walk for a few minutes. I'd better go look for him."

"Take Taylor with you," said Ming. "Darby, Raphael, come with us. We need to be certain that none are still in the house, at least no live ones."

Outside the fence, people were coming onto the street in ones and twos. "The gunfire is over," said Hong. "I suspect the police will be along shortly."

The glow of false dawn showed over the tops of the houses down the street. "Another interesting day, brother," said Ming.

"Yes, another interesting day."

XLII

The police did arrive, but not for another hour. Ming and Hong were waiting at the gate with Taylor and Orville when Harmon arrived. He stared at the gate and chuckled. "I guess somebody brought dynamite this time." He turned to his men. "This is a crime scene. I want you men to cover every inch of this property and every nook and cranny in the house. I want evidence."

"Hold it right there."

Harmon turned and saw a group of men in suits standing beside Judge Werther. The man who spoke stepped forward and opened his coat to show a shield pinned to his vest. "I'm Secret Service Agent Charles Hopkins. We are taking over this investigation." A tarp covered wagon rolled up behind him.

"What?" said Harmon. "You can't just come in here and…"

"Oh yes they can," said Werther. He held up a folded sheaf of paper. "And here is the court order giving them the authority."

Harmon shook his head and put up his hands in a refusing posture. "Oh no, you're not going to push us away again."

"This is now a Federal investigation," said Hopkins.

"On what grounds?" said Harmon, his voice taking on a petulant tone.

"These men operate an international trading and shipping company. We believe this attack is related to the smuggling of contraband between here and Australia."

"That's ridiculous," fumed Harmon. That has nothing to do with…"

"And you know this how?"

Harmon's eyes darted from side.

"Expect a subpoena." said Hopkins. "Now, I'm ordering you and your men to leave this area immediately."

"And if we don't?"

Hopkins stepped back and one of his men pulled the tarp away from the wagon revealing a Gatling gun with an operator seated behind it. "There will be consequences."

The sight of the gun took all of the fight out of Harmon. He walked away and his men followed him, keeping a wary eye on the bore of the machine gun that followed them down the street until they were out of sight.

Werther stepped over to Ming and Hong. "Hell of a thing, but I see you are all right." He saw Taylor's bandaged head and the plaster over Hong's ear. "More or less."

"More than less," said Ming, and Werther smiled.

"We have a man who needs medical attention," said Hong.

"And several who need a hearse."

•••

The newspapers were filled with the story the next day, the official story, that is, dictated by Petterel to his newspaper lap dogs:

A gang of persons unknown, attempted to forcibly enter the home of Ming and Hong Smith, local businessmen and were killed in the attempt. The bodies of the attackers have been taken to the City Repository for autopsy and identification. Further details are not immediately available because Federal officials are investigating the incident for ties to an international smuggling ring.

Darby threw down the paper in disgust. "I wish I was back at the *Chronicle*. I'd've given them the real story."

"If you were still at the *Chronicle*, you wouldn't know the real story," said Ming. "I thought that's why you left them to work for us in the first place."

"You're right." Darby puffed at his cigar for a moment then said, "It is better to know than to report."

"I'll have that carved on your tombstone," said Hong with a laugh.

"Something else did not make the papers," said Ming. "Agent Hopkins said that Ambassador Sen Ti is dead; found murdered in his hotel room. It appears he and his valet had a disagreement that led to their mutual homicide."

"You believe that?" said Darby.

"Not for one second."

"I wonder how Petterel will react," said Hong.

"I'm sure he sent flowers, Darby quipped.

"Have you heard from Chang?" said Ming.

"Yeah. He said that the bounty's lifted from my head and I can walk the streets of Chinatown again."

"I'd give it a week if I were you, Darby, just to let the word get around."

"So what now?"

"Ming and I are going to try to restore our home to its former condition.

We need to consult a landscaper. Instead of a formal British garden, we were thinking of something more continental, say a Renaissance Italian garden."

Darby grinned but kept his thoughts to himself.

XLIII

*L*ater that afternoon the gate bell rang, and from above, the brothers saw Meyung Loo waiting below. The dynamited gate lay twisted to the side, but Meyung was nothing if not an observer of protocol. He stood patiently; his hands folded before him until Raphael walked down the driveway and bade him enter.

In the office, Ming and Hong sat at their desk as Meyung Loo came in. Taylor stood, arms folded over his chest just inside the door. They bowed respectfully to each other and Ming said, "Please sit down. We have much to discuss."

"We are in your debt. We regret the loss of your fellow priest."

Meyung nodded. "He served well and gave his life. No more could be asked of anyone."

"We have found the Eye."

Meyung's head snapped upward. "You found it? You have it?"

"In a hollowed plank in Sing Chung's stolen crate, we found this." Ming put his hand palm down on the desk and when he took it away. The gem shone crimson in the sunlight streaming through the window.

Meyung was motionless for a few seconds, staring at the Eye. Then he slowly rose from his chair and approached it like a man walking in a dream. He took in a breath and let it out, and as he approached the desk, he reached out his hand to touch it, to reassure himself that it was real.

Hong picked up a paperweight, a bronze pyramid and slammed it down on the jewel. He took the pyramid away, and all that remained of the gem was powder.

Meyung's mouth sagged open as his mind caught up with what his eyes had just seen. "What have you done?" he shrieked and tried to climb over the desk, his fingers hooked into claws.

Taylor caught him from behind, wrapping him in a bear hug and pinning his arms. He leaned backward leaving the priest's feet dangling.

"I am sorry, Meyung Loo," said Hong in Mandarin. "What you saw was not the Eye. I apologize for shocking you in this way, but we had to know whether you knew that what we were chasing was not really the Eye of Quang-Chi but an artful imitation."

Meyung stopped struggling. "Taylor, please set him down."

The priest stood still, eyes fixed on the crushed jewel. "An imitation? I do not understand."

"We have all been the victims of an elaborate ruse," said Hong. "You and your brothers, Sing Chung, the Tong, the Sons of Thunder, and I regret to say, ourselves as well."

"The jewel that was smuggled from your land to ours was nothing more than paste and dye," Ming said, running his hands through the colored dust. "It was treated as if it were the real Eye, because everyone who took part in the scheme believed it was so, except the person who set it in motion."

Tong said, "We have reason to believe that Sen Ti, the Emperor's ambassador, has fabricated this entire scheme. He paid the traitor in your brotherhood to steal the Eye and had a copy made by a skilled artisan. He then made arrangements with the Tong in China to smuggle it to America in Sing Chung's crate. There, their operatives in Chinatown would retrieve what they believed was the real gem. Meanwhile, while your people pursued the gem, and the Customs agents on both continents were watching the Tong, Sen Ti took advantage of his diplomatic status to smuggled the real Eye into America in his diplomatic pouch."

"But circumstance intervened and spoiled the plan," Ming went on. "The Parma Queen arrived early and the Tong were not in place to intercept the crate. A man named Won Lao stole the crate at random from the dock, and the plot began to unravel. The theft was discovered by Sing Chung, who tried to enlist our help in finding the crate. When the Tong discovered the crate was gone, they began an all out search for it, knowing there would be hell to pay if they didn't find the gem.

"They found Won Lao before our operatives did, and with him the crate. They tortured him to death, but Won Lao did not tell them what they wanted to know because he did not know it himself. It seems that Sing Chung was playing his own game. Instead of hiding the Eye in the terra cotta horse as he was told to do, he had a secret compartment built into a board of the crate. The Tong killed him before he could reveal this fact; after all, he believed the crate stolen and the Eye lost forever.

"We took the crate apart and after considerable examination, located the secret compartment and the gem, but from the moment we saw it, my brother and I suspected that it was not real. We ran tests to determine its verity and found that our suspicions were right, but we did not tell even our associates what we had learned."

"But where is the Eye now?" said Meyung.

"That we do not know. I fear it is lost forever," said Hong.

"Then I have failed my people."

"Perhaps not," said Ming. "Belief is a powerful force if you can convey it to others." He opened a drawer of the desk and removed a black velvet pouch. He opened it and set on his desk another gem identical to the Eye. "This replica will not shatter so easily. It was made by one of the best counterfeit jewelers in the world to our specification. If you take it back to your people, who is to say it is not the real Eye?"

Meyung Loo became indignant. "You would have me deceive my people?"

"How many people have died because they believed the false Eye to be the real one? How many of your people will live free because they believe?"

"The Emperor's star is fading in the light of a new dawn," said Hong. "And now we must discuss the secret you have kept from us. You will see your friends the Righteous Fists triumph if their faith does not falter. It is for them you wish your people to stand against the Emperor, is it not?"

Meyung was silent for a moment. "Yes. It is true. They grow in numbers and strength and we believe they will save us from the western world our greedy leaders, men like Sen Ti are so determined to embrace; their culture, their fashion, their religions."

"I hope you understand that we have acted on your behalf, although to promote the Boxer cause is to act against our own interests. Closing trade to the West will harm our company as much as any in San Francisco."

"You have acted honorably and are a credit to your ancestors," said Meyung.

"There is one more item," said Hong. "Since we failed to return the real Eye of Quang-Chi to you, we cannot rightfully keep your payment." He set the pouch of gold dust on the desk. "Please, take it and use it for the good of your people."

Meyung Loo rose and bowed to the brothers. They bowed in return, and the priest left without another word.

Ming and Hong returned to their chalkboard. They studied the diagram for a moment, then Ming picked up the eraser and rubbed out Sen Ti's circle. Then, he rubbed out Meyung Loo's circle.

"One loose end to tie."

XLIV

*T*aylor pulled the carriage to the entrance of City Hall. Ming and Hong climbed down and Hong told him, "There will be no need to wait for us, Taylor. Please take the carriage home. If we do not return or contact you by two o'clock," he handed an envelope to Taylor. "Deliver this to Judge Werther immediately, and wait for his instructions."

Taylor looked puzzled. "Uh, okay. But how will you get home?"

"We may not be going home today," said Ming.

"I don't understand."

"Better that you do not. Then you cannot be deemed an accomplice. Go." And the brothers climbed the stairs to the tall bronze doors like a man on his way to the gallows, leaving Taylor staring after them.

The twins climbed the steps to the second floor in perfect time with each other. The few people in the building through the lunch hour stared after them as they passed by. The door to Petterel's anteroom was open, and through the doorway, Ming and Hong saw the pretty red-haired girl struggling with one of the new typewriters, something acquired since the last time they were in the office. They continued down the hallway to the Recorder of Deeds Office and waited long enough for the suspicious to believe that that was where they intended to go.

As they entered Petterel's anteroom, the red haired girl smiled broadly. Although she had seen the brothers before, they were still a curiosity. "Good afternoon, gentlemen, may I help you?"

"Good afternoon, Miss," said Ming, bowing slightly. "Is Commissioner Petterel in?"

"Yes, sir," she said. "He's busy at the moment. Shall I tell him you're here?"

"Don't bother," said Hong. "Tell me Miss," he read her name plate, "Davis, have you had your lunch yet?"

"Uh no. Why?"

"Because Lorimar's has a wonderful steak and champagne special. I'm sure you would enjoy it." He laid a fifty dollar bill on her desk just out of her reach.

She smiled coyly this time. "I'd have to be back by one."

"Of course. I'm sure there will be plenty of time."

Miss Davis put her hand over the bill and curled her fingers, folding it in half and half again. She slipped it up the cuff of her sleeve as naturally as if she'd done it every day of the week, which perhaps she did for anyone who came to see the Commissioner on "official business."

She stood and pushed back her chair. "Thanks for the tip. I'm sure I'll enjoy it." She slipped on her gloves, picked up her handbag, and left the room.

The brothers quietly closed the outer door and set the lock. They turned the knob and walked unannounced into Petterel's office.

The Commissioner sat behind his desk, a file open before him. He was in shirtsleeves, his jacket draped over the arm of one of the leather chairs near his desk. The brothers stood, their gloved hands resting on the heads of their canes.

He looked startled, then wary, then angry at their intrusion. "What are you doing here? Who told you that you could come into this office?"

"This is a public building, and you are a public official," said Ming. "The last time I heard, we are still a part of the public."

"Before I have you thrown out, I may as well ask you, what the hell do you want?"

"Simply to talk," Hong said.

"Talk. About what?"

"About why my brother and I are being persecuted by the City Police Force."

"We would ask Sergeant Hawkins, but we haven't seen him in the building today."

Petterel's face reddened. "You were told to lay off the case with the priests. You didn't. Don't whine to me about the consequences."

"Ah yes, that word. Consequences, You did say there would be consequences. Did that apply to your friend Sen Ti? Consequences?"

Petterel's knuckles whitened on the edge of his desk.

"We understand that the Ambassador met an untimely end, along with his valet. Of what behavior were those events consequences?"

"Get out." Petterel hissed.

"One last question, Commissioner. Who will your new partners be in Empire Shipping, now that Sen Ti is gone and Hawkins is no longer able to serve as Chairman of the Directors?"

"You think you know so much, but you know nothing."

"We know that you and Sing Chung have a shared past, and that Sing Chung smuggled a very valuable stolen gem into our port on behalf of the Tong, and that the gem went missing, causing a frenzy among the underworld of Chinatown, and all for an imitation ruby."

Petterel turned pale. He stood and picked up his coat from the chair. He thrust one arm into a sleeve then the other.

"Are you leaving, Commissioner?" said Ming. "We were just getting started."

"No, and neither are you." He reached into his coat, and when he pulled a small caliber pistol from his pocket, the brothers understood why he put it on. "Do you know Sen Ti offered me ten thousand dollars to kill the two of you, but I told him I'd have it done for free, because you two have been a thorn in my side for years, nosing into cases I could have easily closed to the benefit of one party or another and undoing well-laid plans."

"They do 'gang aft a-gley'", said Hong.

Petterel opened a drawer in his desk. He took out a second pistol and laid it on his blotter. "You have no idea what your interference has destroyed."

"An international smuggling ring with you turning the eye of the police away here while Sen Ti did so at the other end in Shanghai? Corruption at the highest level," Ming said.

Hong asked, "What was it you thought to smuggle between here and China? Opium? Prostitutes? Weapons?"

"Anything we wanted. The pressure was on the Emperor to suspend trade with the West, to stop the flow of Western ideas along with Western goods. Sen Ti had the Emperor's ear. We would have been one of a handful of companies trading with China and have had a free hand to transport whatever we chose. But that's all done now. Years of planning and execution finished, largely because of you."

"So many deaths," said Ming, "and you would add two more souls to your burden?"

"Souls? You two are an abomination. You haven't one soul between you let alone two. I'll kill you and shoot a hole in the wall with the other pistol and put it in your hand. You sneak into my office, threaten me with a gun, and I shoot you in self-defense. No jury in America would convict me of killing two half-breed monsters, let alone in San Francisco. And your accusations? Hearsay. Slander. There is no tangible proof."

"That may be so, Petterel." said Hong, "but there will be no justice while you yet live."

The brothers took a step toward him and Petterel pulled the trigger. The little pistol boomed loudly in the small room. The shot struck Ming and Hong in their connecting trunk, rocking them backward, but the small caliber bullet failed to penetrate the bone over their heart.

Hong raised his hand and pointed an accusing finger at Petterel. The 32 caliber pistol in his glove cracked like miniature thunderclap. Years of marksmanship training paid off. Hong had to fire only one shot. It struck Petterel in the center of his forehead and left a perfectly round hole like a blind third eye. He slumped forward over the arm of the leather chair.

The brothers heard running feet, frantic pounding at the outer door, then breaking glass as the upper panel of the door was shattered and the lock turned. Hong pulled off his glove and laid the smoking pistol on Petterel's desk. When the officers rushed into the inner office with their guns drawn, they saw Ming and Hong standing quietly, hands in the air.

"I have shot the Commissioner. I surrender," said Hong. "Please do not harm my brother."

XLV

*M*ing and Hong were handcuffed and marched out through the anteroom where the shards of door glass lay on the floor, the letters that once spelled "Robert Petterel, Commissioner of Police" scattered at random.

Hong looked at the gold leaf letters at his feet and said, "All the King's horses and all the King's men."

Hundreds of people mobbed the sidewalk as the brothers were marched down the City Hall steps and loaded into a paddy wagon. Magnesium flashed as photographers captured the arrest on silver nitrate. Reporters shouted unanswered questions at the brothers and the police, and people craned their necks for a look at the killer.

The crowd trailed after the wagon as it made its way slowly through the crowded streets and followed it to the precinct station. Otherwise, it may have taken the brothers a completely different direction, never to be seen again. The wagon was backed up to the rear door of the station and the brothers were roughly hauled from the wagon into the hallway and directly to a holding cell.

There they sat for nearly an hour until a familiar face appeared: Detective Harmon. "Well, well. Your federal friends can't get you out of this one." He leered through the bars. "I've got you two on first degree murder."

"No, Detective," said Hong. "My brother did not kill Petterel. I did."

"You're one person as far as I'm concerned. And that's how a jury will see it too. I'll hang you in tandem," Harmon gloated," or maybe I'll flip a coin to see who goes first; hang one of you and let the other one watch him die, then finish the job."

"We have been shot, Detective. We need medical attention."

"You look okay to me," Harmon sneered.

"May we see a lawyer?" said Ming.

"You'll see a lawyer when I say you can see a lawyer. This ain't Angle Street, fellas."

An officer came up behind Harmon and whispered in his ear. "Stall them." To the turnkey, he said, "Open the cell. We're taking them elsewhere."

Ming said quietly to Hong, "I think the Judge has arrived."

The brothers were yanked to their feet and half-carried down the hallway to the waiting paddy wagon. The streets were less crowded now and the ride was faster and rougher, bouncing them against the walls of the wagon and once onto the floor between the benches. When the wagon stopped, it was a blessing.

Wherever they were, it was dark. There was no sound but rain falling and the rustle of tree branches in a stiff wind. Ming and Hong were dragged across a muddy yard and up a set of wooden steps into a sort of cabin that smelled of mildew and rot.

Someone lit a lamp. The room was about ten feet square and empty of furniture except for a table and a few old wooden chairs that looked as if they would fly apart if someone sat in them. The walls were open joists with rough planks nailed over the outside. Ominous dark stains covered large areas of the rough plank floor.

"Welcome to the Ritz, boys," said one of the uniforms and the other two guffawed. "This is the accommodation for special prisoners." He had a gap between his teeth and a wart on his nose; incredibly, he also wore a wedding ring. He shoved them roughly. "Sit down." They sat against the wall, legs splayed outward. The other two coppers grabbed their manacles by the chains and pulled them upward; hanging them by iron hooks 'til their toes barely touched the floor.

"We'll come back later, if we feel like it," the gap-toothed cop said. He blew out the lamp, and he and his friends walked out the door, bolting it behind them. Seconds later, the brothers heard the sounds of heavy blows and falling bodies. The door swung open and a voice called, "Sirs, are you in here?"

"Raphael," said Ming. "Yes. We're here. Light the lamp."

In the lamplight, the brothers saw Raphael and Taylor behind him, a pick handle in his hand. He set it against the wall and began dragging the three unconscious policemen through the cabin door.

"How did you find us, Taylor?" said Hong.

"That federal agent—Hopkins? He said that I was to follow the paddy wagon and never lose sight of it in case they tried to move you where we couldn't help. As soon as I saw it was rolling out of town, I knew they weren't taking you home."

Raphael was rifling the cops' pockets. "Here is the key to the manacles." Taylor lifted the brothers bodily and slipped their handcuffs off the hooks. As Raphael unlocked the cuffs, one of the cops groaned and stirred. Taylor bent down and grabbed him by the hair and slammed his forehead on the rough floorboards then did it again for good measure. If the man were still awake, he had sense enough not to move again.

"Help me tie these three up," Taylor said to Raphael. He bound them hand and foot and instead of hanging their hands over the hooks, he hung them by their feet.

"Take their badges." Hong stood rubbing his wrists. "They have individual numbers."

"Yes," said Ming. "We will have proof that we were abducted and abused, and by whom."

Taylor tore the badges from the officers' tunics and stuffed them into the pocket of his coat.

"I'm going to tie the draft horses to the back of the carriage. I'll turn them loose a few miles away, just in case those three wake up and figure out a way to escape. Let them walk back to Frisco. It's only twelve miles."

"Well, Taylor," said Hong. "I suppose that in spite of our good intentions you're an accessory anyway."

Taylor grinned. "Boss, I wouldn't have it any other way."

Taylor let the horses go at a crossroads three or four miles from the cabin. He slapped them on the rump, sending one in one direction and its partner the other. They drove through the pelting rain, Taylor under an oil skin slicker and Raphael and the brothers huddled under the landau roof. After an hour lights became more frequent and the pavement became regular. Soon they were rolling along the edge of the bay.

Taylor wheeled the carriage onto a pier and reined the horses to a stop. He jumped down and stood beside the horses waving one of the small lamps from the side of the carriage. A light waved in answer, and in a moment, two of the Secret Service agents the brothers recognized from

"Take their badges," Hong stood rubbing his writsts.

the raid on the mansion appeared, holding their hats onto their heads in the wind.

Taylor stuck his head into the carriage. "This is Agent Barlow. The other fellow is agent Travis. They're going to take you to safety."

"Safety?" said Ming. "I didn't think any place in San Francisco would be safe."

"Only one, Mister Smith," said Travis. "You're going into protective custody. We're taking you to the military prison on Alcatraz."

"Taylor," said Hong. "You and Darby. See to it that Miss Donatelli is protected."

"Yes, Boss. We will."

The small steam launch pitched so high in the waves as they sailed past the breakwater that Ming and Hong wondered whether they might have been safer taking their chances with the San Francisco Police.

"Agent Travis," shouted Ming into his ear, "I must tell you, we can't swim very well."

Travis thought about it for a few seconds and pulled a life preserver from its mount on a bulkhead of the launch. "Take this," Travis said. "If you go overboard, just hang onto it. It should float you both."

As they neared the island prison, the storm intensified and jagged lightning etched the sky, highlighting the grim pile of stone that was the world's most inescapable prison. The agents tied the launch to the pier and helped the brothers out of the rocking craft and onto the dock. "This way, gentlemen. Warden Grenfell is waiting."

Jonathan Grenfell was a short man but his thick chest, muscular arms and bull neck testified to his physical strength. His thick shock of grey hair spilled from halfway back his scalp to his shirt collar. "Like Theseus, gentlemen," he joked. Nothing for an enemy to grab in front and I'll never turn my back for one to grab me from behind."

He led them into his office, a pleasantly fitted room in a grim place. "Would you like brandy, or whiskey perhaps, take the chill off?"

"Brandy would be most welcome," said Hong. Ming nodded agreement.

"I've been in contact with Judge Werther," said Grenfell. He has asked that you be extended every courtesy while you are here. I am making my personal quarters available for you until we have a suitable room of your own—without bars." He laughed. "I understand you may be staying with us for a while, the court system being what it is."

"Not to disparage your hospitality, Warden, but I hope it is not too long a while." Ming smiled. "And by the way, this is excellent brandy."

"Unfortunately, this is a prison and it must be run as such. I can afford you a fair degree of freedom on the Rock—that's what the inmates call it—but there are limits for your safety and our security."

"We will cooperate in every way, sir," said Ming. "We are grateful for your hospitality."

"I hope you still feel the same in a week or so."

XLVI

*T*wo days later, Ming and Hong were moved into a pair of rooms in the guards' quarters where they could comfortably wait for their court appearance. Raphael came with clothing, books and other items to normalize their stay, including Ming's flute and Hong's cello. He also brought their correspondence, and on two occasions, Albert Foster with the ledgers from Oriental Trading.

Three weeks to the day since they set foot on the Rock, Judd Wilson, the attorney Judge Werther hired to represent them, arrived with a date for their trial.

"The Judge and I give the strategy you suggest a fifty-fifty chance at best," Wilson said, "but if that's how you want to play it, I'll honor your wishes. The newspapers are screaming for your heads, yelling about the privileged rich."

"And ignoring the wealth their elected officials rake into their coffers from graft and kickbacks?"

"I can say only that at the moment, public opinion has been working against you because all they hear is what pours out of City Hall."

"Let Darby handle that end of things at the time of the trial," said Ming. "Now, let us go over your brief."

That night the brothers stood on a promontory overlooking the bay and saw the twinkling lights of the city across the dark water.

"It's a strange feeling," said Ming, "as if we've been disowned by our country."

"Yes, but perhaps San Francisco will prove a forgiving city."

Both were silent for a moment. Finally, Ming said, "You're thinking about Maria."

"As are you."

Ming nodded. "If we win our freedom, can we stay in San Francisco, and would it be fair to ask her to come with us to another place?"

"Nothing in life is fair beyond what we choose for ourselves. She will decide, and we will abide by her decision."

"'It is ironic, is it not, that we are prisoners already and haven't even come to trial."

Hong nodded. "But we are alive."

XLVII

Raphael stayed in the prison the night before the trial to help the brothers prepare in the morning. They dressed in grey suits with a fine dark pinstripe, white shirts with wing collars, and wine red stocks. High button shoes with spats and Derby hats completed their dress.

Grenfell was waiting at the dock when they arrived to board the launch. "Can't complain about the weather," he said, pointing to the cloudless sky and the bright sun. He shook hands with the brothers and said simply, "Good luck."

"With good luck, we'll be free today, and not trouble you again."

"Come back any time," Grenfell said with a chuckle. "Just not in leg irons."

The launch was supposed to dock at a private mooring away from crowds and reporters, but someone leaked the location, and when the brothers climbed out of the launch, they were met by a torrent of questions, the flash of photographers, and a mixture of encouragement and taunting from a crowd that threatened to spill over the side of the dock and into the ocean.

The police pushed the crowd back to let the brothers pass, and they were loaded into a closed wagon with two armed guards and driven to the County Court House. The carriage delivered the brothers to a rear entrance so that the mob scene at the dock was not repeated. Judd Wilson and Judge Werther were waiting. They were taken through a maze of passages that led ultimately into the courtroom of the Honorable Judge Homer L. Bennet.

As soon as the brothers entered the courtroom, the crowds in the gallery erupted in a roar. Some shouted "cop-killers", some shouted "Killer cops."

"You've caused quite a controversy," said Werther. "I haven't seen a crowd so divided since the abolition of slavery."

Arthur Gillette of the District Attorney's office walked in accompanied by two of his staffers and Detective Harmon, who glared at them and mouthed a few unintelligible words at the brothers before he sat at the Prosecution's table.

The bailiff entered the room and began his "Oyez Oyez" speech and had to stop because he couldn't be heard. The court constables quieted the gallery. When he said, "All rise," the hubbub started again. Judge Bennet took his seat and picked up his gavel. He pounded it for order and when the noise died down, he said, "I will have order in this courtroom, and ensure that end..." He gestured to the bailiff who opened a door to chambers, and twelve Sheriff's deputies filed in, truncheons in hand. Four of them remained on the floor, and the rest climbed the stairs to the gallery.

"I have authorized these deputies to maintain order by whatever force necessary, and that includes dragging you down the stairs and throwing you out into the street. I sincerely hope we understand each other. Call the case."

The bailiff read, "The State of California versus Hong Smith on a charge of murder in the first degree."

"How does the defendant plead?"

"If it please the Court, your Honor, at this time, Defense would petition the Court to quash the indictments against both of these men." The gallery began to rumble.

Gillette leaped to his feet. "That's outrageous. On what grounds?"

Bennet slammed his gavel like a pistol shot. "Mister Gillette, I will ask such questions, and I will determine what constitutes 'outrageous' in this courtroom. Your office entitles you exactly the same consideration as the gallery in my deployment of these constables. Am I clear?"

Gillette swallowed visibly and took a deep breath before answering. "Yes, your Honor. I apologize to the Court."

"Don't let it happen again. There are too any short fuses today already, and I expect counsel on both sides," he looked pointedly at Wilson, "to set a proper example of deportment. Now, Counselor, on what grounds do you offer this petition?"

"Your honor, Defense believes that a guilty verdict in this case would lead to cruel and unusual punishment."

Gillette looked ready to jump to his feet again, but instead gripped the table with both hands.

"Counselor," said Bennet, "we routinely hang murderers in California. I feel reasonably certain you know that."

"With all due respect, your honor, if you hang Hong Smith for the murder of Robert Petterel, you will be murdering an innocent man, his conjoined brother Ming Smith, and Defense is prepared to provide argument and evidence to that fact."

Gillette jumped to his feet. "Objection!"

"Overruled. I want to hear this argument. Proceed, Mister Wilson."

"My clients are, as all of San Francisco knows, conjoined twins. Their unique circumstance makes it impossible to put one to death without killing the other. I would ask the Court's permission to call as a witness Doctor Richard Feverell."

"Granted," said Bennet.

Feverell put his hand on the Bible. Wilson had chosen him because he was every bit the picture of the benign family physician; grey hair, moustache, and rimless eyeglasses down his nose. The bailiff swore him in and he took the seat, smiling.

"Doctor Feverell, have you met the accused, Hong and Ming Smith?"

"Yes I have."

"Have you examined them in your professional capacity as a physician?"

"Yes, I have."

"And apart from their obvious conjointure, do Ming and Hong Smith exhibit any other medical, shall we say, oddities?"

"They share a heart and one lung."

The crowd began to murmur and Bennet rapped his gavel.

"If one were to die, what would happen to the other?"

"Death would follow soon after to the other as the body of the dead twin broke down and polluted their shared blood with necrotic cells."

"So, to execute Hong Smith would surely mean the execution of Ming Smith as well."

"I believe so, yes."

"Thank you, Doctor. No further questions. Mister Gillette, your witness."

Gillette approached the witness box as he might a dog in his flower bed. "Doctor Feverell, how many years have you practiced medicine?"

"Thirty-two years next January."

"And in that time, have you ever treated conjoined twins other than The Smith Brothers?"

"You call them Ming and Hong to show them as individuals," whispered Werther to Wilson. "He calls them the Smith Brothers treating them as a unit. Work that, Judd. Make him use their individual names."

"No," said Feverell. "Ming and Hong Smith are the first."

"Then with all due respect, sir, how can you hold yourself as an expert on the subject? How can you say with certainty that to kill one would kill the other?"

"Objection. The Prosecution is asking multiple questions."

"Sustained. Counselor, please ask the witness one thing at a time."

Gillette took a deep breath and let it out slowly. "Doctor, what leads you to believe that to kill Hong Smith would be to kill his brother as well?"

"Medical precedent sir."

"And what precedent might that be?"

The most famous conjoined twins in the world, Chang and Eng Bunker, P. T. Barnum's Siamese Twins. On January seventh, 1874, Chang died of a severe case of bronchitis. Eng died within two hours of his brother's passing, and they did not even share a heart."

Gillette's face fell. "No further questions."

The second witness was Edward Thompson, a guard at City Hall, who was first in the room when Petterel was killed.

"Officer Thompson, on the date in question, what did you see when you entered Robert Petterel's office?"

"I saw Commissioner Petterel, of course, slumped over a chair, and I saw the Smith Brothers."

"And what were Ming and Hong Smith doing?"

"Nothing. They were standing still with their hands in the air."

"I see. And did either of them say anything?"

"The one on the left said, 'I shot the Commissioner. I surrender. Please do not harm my brother.'"

"Would you please point out for the Court which of these men you mean when you say 'the one on the left'?"

"Him."

"Let the record show that then witness has indicated Hong Smith."

"Objection, Your Honor, this is moot. Hong Smith has admitted the killing of Robert Petterel."

"Overruled. I am intrigued, Mister Wilson, by your line of reasoning. Please tell where it is going."

"I will, Your Honor. Officer Thompson, did you see any weapons in the room?"

"Yes. There were three pistols."

"Where were they located?"

"One on the floor beside Commissioner Petterel and two on the desk."

"Was anyone injured other than Mister Petterel?"

"The Smith Brothers were bleeding from a wound to the chest."

"Would you say, then, that Mister Petterel and Hong Smith shot each other?"

"Objection! Defense is leading the witness."

"Sustained."

"I withdraw the question. I would point to the police report. It states that Mister Petterel was shot by the same caliber pistol found on the desk near Hong Smith, and Hong and Ming Smith were shot by the same caliber pistol as that found beside Mister Petterel."

"Objection!" Gillette could hardly contain himself. "Who is testifying here, Your Honor, the witness of Counsel for the Defense."

"I will overrule that objection, Mister Gillette. That information is germane to any decision I will make on the matter. Please sit down." Gillette was fuming now.

"Defense maintains, Your Honor, that Hong Smith admittedly killed Robert Petterel. Whether it is a case of murder or self-defense is an issue for a jury. My contention remains that should Hong Smith be found guilty, to execute him would be a case of the State murdering an innocent man."

"He didn't pull the trigger, but he was in on it." Gillette shouted.

"Your Honor, Ming Smith is not on trial here. Hong Smith is. To find Hong Smith guilty would send him to the gallows and his brother, yet to be found guilty of anything would die with him."

"They're one. They live together, they act together."

"Mister Gillette, this is your final warning."

"If it please the Court, Your Honor, may I propose a simple demonstration to prove that Ming and Hong Smith are indeed two separate personalities?"

"We've gone this far. Let's see it through to the end."

Two chairs were set before the bench, and Ming and Hong were sworn in.

"Your Honor," said Wilson, "I have in my hand this morning's *San Francisco Chronicle.* I am going to give one page to Hong Smith and one to Ming Smith. Have you gentlemen seen today's newspaper?"

Both said no.

"Then there is no way that either or both of you could have in any way memorized the content of any page of this newspaper."

He handed one page to Ming and the other to Hong. "Please read aloud from your page. The brothers began reading two different articles at the same time.

"That will do, gentlemen, thank you." Wilson turned to the bench. "Your Honor, I believe that this adequately demonstrates that Ming and

Hong Smith are perfectly capable of acting independently. They are two separate personalities despite their physical conjointure, and to punish both for the independent action of one is not only illegal, it is immoral. I therefore respectfully request that you quash this indictment and let these men go. They have suffered enough."

Wilson turned and tucked the *Chronicle* under his arm leaving the headline visible for all to see: Petterel Implicated in International Smuggling Scheme, Darby's article under another reporter's byline.

"Mister Gillette, do you have anything further?"

"No, Your Honor, except to say that I believe it would be a gross miscarriage of justice to allow these men, who have murdered a trusted public servant, to walk free from this court room."

"Noted. I will take some time to ponder this matter, and I will reconvene at one o'clock this afternoon." Bennet rapped his gavel. "Adjourned until one o'clock."

XLVIII

The next two hours passed as slowly for Ming and Hong as had any in their lives. At five minutes to one, the bailiff came for them and they returned to their chairs at the defense table.

"All rise."

Judge Bennet took his seat and waited for the murmur of the crowd to die down. "I have carefully considered the testimony given here today, and I must say, I wrestled with the problem like Jacob with the angel. Mister Wilson has rightly pointed out that only one of the Smith Brothers is on trial today, and to send him to the gallows would end his untried brother's life as well. A law that punishes the innocent is no law at all. I hereby declare the indictments in both cases quashed. You men are free to go. Case dismissed."

"The courtroom exploded in cheers and jeers. Bennet said "Court adjourned," but no one heard him. Gillette sat with his head in his hands.

Harmon pushed his way through the throng of well wishers to stand inches from the Brothers and say through clenched teeth, "This isn't over."

"Harmon," said Hong, "it is never over."

XLIX

The brothers stood before the pier glass in their bedroom, Hong inserting the onyx studs in his pleated shirt front, and Ming adjusting the suspenders on his tuxedo trousers. It had been almost a month since the trial, and the furor had all but died. A few editorials about the privilege of the wealthy still alluded to Petterel's killing, but most of the press now concerned itself with the upcoming mayoral race. The most amusing of the rants after the trial was a piece in which the anonymous author alluded to the case in terms of the "Yellow Peril" and the "Chinese problem," completely overlooking the fact that Ming and Hong were born American citizens.

"Tonight will be interesting," said Ming, buttoning the last strap of his suspenders.

"Indeed." Hong replied, slipping in his cuff links. "I am curious to see how Society regards us; as the unpunished murderers of a trusted public servant, or as the slayers of a dark knight?"

"As in any trial, someone is always disappointed at the outcome."

"Instead of being judged by our enemies, perhaps we should be judged by those scandalized at our acquittal."

"In any event, I think we did the right thing in accepting the invitation."

The Star Ball was one of San Francisco's most anticipated charity events in recent years, patronized by the cream of Society and celebrities of every stripe. Proceeds went to a number of local causes and institutions to help the poor, the ill and the lame. Since dancing was not their favorite activity, the brothers had attended only once before, although they had been invited every year since.

Raphael entered with their shoes polished to a high gloss. "Will there be anything else, sirs?"

"Thank you, no, Raphael," said Ming. "We can manage from here."

They sat to slip on the black leather pumps with the grosgrain edges and bows.

"Who decided what constitutes proper formal wear?" said Hong.

"The same person who decided that Masons should wear ritual aprons and Scotsmen should wear kilts."

Downstairs, Raphael gave their tail coats a last brushing and helped them into the cape. The last touch was the high silk hats, which each set carefully on his head at just the right angle.

"Are we presentable, Raphael?" said Ming.

Raphael blinked with surprise. In all the years he had served the Smith Brothers, neither had ever asked him such a question. "Why, yes, sirs. Eminently so."

"Then let us go."

Raphael opened the doors and they found Taylor waiting with the coach. The climbed in, and as the coach rolled down the drive, Hong said. "Are you that uncertain about this evening? You've never asked Raphael's opinion on anything in your life. Maybe you should ask Taylor what he thinks.

"Raphael is a gentlemen's gentleman. He knows fashion. Taylor is not clothed, he is upholstered."

The facade of the Royal Hotel was ablaze with lights and carriages jockeyed for position to pull to the curb so that bejeweled women and tuxedoed men could step from them and cross the brilliant red carpet to the hotel's entrance. The rich, the powerful, the famous, and the notorious all came out in their finery to see and be seen by those whom they saw as peers.

Liveried footmen opened carriage doors, and uniformed doormen bowed at the waist as the guests paraded inside.

Taylor pulled the carriage to the curb and one of the footmen let down the steps. The brothers sidled to the carpet, and the excited chatter faded from the nearest to the farthest as the crowd saw the infamous Smith Brothers. Holding their heads high, gold-topped canes in hand, Ming and Hong strode down the carpet and the hubbub grew like the sound of a rainstorm from the first few drops to a downpour.

The *maitre d'hôtel*, dressed in waistcoat, breeches, and a powdered wig, stood at the entrance of the ball room, announcing guests as they arrived and guiding them to the receiving line, the Barretts, the Hodgsons, the Livengoods, America's closest analog to royalty. He pounded his mace on the ball room floor and boomed out, "Messers Ming Smith and Hong Smith." The orchestra had just finished a song, and in the sudden absence of music, the announcement seemed almost harsh.

Ming and Hong stood at the entrance and stared around the room at the crowd, frozen in mid gesture, mouths open but not speaking. Then across the dance floor, one person began clapping his hands, then another, then two more, until the room was filled with thunderous applause.

Ming and Hong bowed gracefully at the waist and each raised a hand in acknowledgment. The orchestra struck up "The Blue Danube," and the moment was over, but the evening had just begun.

Ming saw her first. Maria crossed the dance floor, oblivious to the twirling couples all around her. Then Hong saw her as well. She was breathtaking in a blue silk gown that flattered her figure, a gossamer white shawl across her bare shoulders. Her hair was swept up in a Spanish style and held by the golden comb the brothers had imported for her from Japan. They had bought the entire stock of them and melted down all but one so that Maria would have the only one in the world. But it was not her clothing nor her hair that the brothers saw, it was her loving smile as she approached.

"I believe this is our dance," Maria said. holding both hands palms forward. The brothers each took a hand in one of theirs and put the other at Maria's waist. They glided gracefully onto the floor, and as they danced, one by one, the other couples stopped and watched in amazement, until the waltz was theirs alone. The three smiled into each other's eyes, grateful that in a world filled with violence, crime, and ugliness, there could yet be moments of sheer beauty.

The End

ABOUT OUR CREATORS

AUTHOR —

FRED ADAMS - is a western Pennsylvania native who has enjoyed a lifelong love affair with horror, fantasy, and science fiction literature and films. He holds a Ph.D. in American Literature from Duquesne University and recently retired from teaching writing and literature in the English Department of Penn State University.

He has published over 50 short stories in amateur, and professional magazines as well as hundreds of news features as a staff writer and sportswriter for the now Pittsburgh Tribune-Review. In the 1970s Fred published the fanzine Spoor and its companion The Spoor Anthology. Hitwolf, Six-Gun Terror and C.O. Jones, Mobsters and Monsters were his first three books for Airship 27, and his novel Dead Man's Melody, another Airship 27 publication, was nominated Best Pulp Novel of the Year for the 2017 Pulp Factory Awards.

ARTIST—

MORGAN FITZSIMONS - is a British artist, illustrator and author. Born in the North of England in 1939, she studied at Liverpool John Moores University, and taught for twenty years. Inspired by W.B. Yeats, Tolkien, CS Lewis, and of course the art of Frank Frazetta, Jim Fitzpatrick and others, her own work has been displayed all over the world. She just finished the cover for Amber Tears, by Jilly Paddock, and is currently working on artwork for a special edition of her novel, The Last Enchanter, and its two sequels. She is fascinated by the ancient myths and legends of our culture, Celtic, Norse and Anglo Saxon, which filters into her work.

OTHER BOOKS BY FRED ADAMS JR.

SIX-GUN TERRORS Vol One
     ISBN-13: 978-0692269732
     ISBN-10: 0692269738
SIX-GUN TERRORS   Vol Two
     ISBN-13: 978-0692479780
     ISBN-10: 0692479783

HITWOLF
     ISBN-13: 978-0692250839
     ISBN-10: 0692250832
HITWOLF 2 – The Pack
     ISBN-13: 978-0997786835
     ISBN-10: 0997786833

C.O. JONES
     ISBN-13: 978-0692483589
     ISBN-10: 0692483586

(SAM DUNNE MYSTERIES)
DEAD MAN'S MELODY
     ISBN-13: 978-0997786859
     ISBN-10: 099778685X

TERROR ON THE PLAINS

Former Union scouts and saddle tramps Durken and McAfee are more than satisfied with their lives as cattle-punchers for Homer Eldridge and his Triple Six ranch. But fate has other, more sinister and weird plans for the two cowpokes...

Writer Fred Adams, Jr. spins weird western tales that will have readers on their edge of their seats and jumping at shadows. Mixing a heady brew that is half H.P. Lovecraft and half Louis L'Amour, SIX-GUN TERRORS volumes one and two are creepy adventures not soon forgotten.

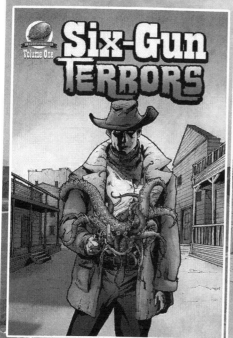